The Elevator Operator
A Modern Fairy Tale
By Barry McMahon

The Elevator Operator: A Modern Fairy Tale
©2020 Barry McMahon

This book is a work of fictional satire. Any resemblance to individuals living or dead is coincidental. Any persons mentioned in the text are objects of parody and are not intended to represent the actual individuals.

ISBN 13: **978-0-9960215-4-8**

Dedication

This book is dedicated to Colleen McMahon, who has constantly encouraged me. Her perseverance in the face of life's trials is pure inspiration. She brings joy to those around her and I hope she feels that joy returned in equal abundance.

Contents

Foreword

Upon reading an old fairy tale, one is presented with absurdity. Assumptions are made about what is good and what is evil, but how different is that from life? It is arguable that neither can exist without the other.

Chapter 1

Eli was born with a caul. Eli's parents were told that this was a sign of great fortune. They received this information at a fair, for a small, suggested donation of twenty-five dollars. Offered entirely as a bonus, included at no extra charge, was a vision of Eli being married to the daughter of a wealthy business mogul by the name of Brian McDonald. A prophecy Eli's parents disregarded.

Brian McDonald had made his fortune by preying on others. He was a big man who had played some football in college but never showed enough promise to go on to the pros. For those who heard him tell the tales, however, it would be difficult to separate his prowess as a lineman from the likes of Hall of Famers Alan Page or Randy White. He had dark hair that he styled after Ronald Reagan, a man he had the utmost respect for. His physical features were classically attractive, apart from his ridiculously small nose, the size of which seemed more appropriate to that of a toddler. This was not a barrier to establishing relationships with women, which he did throughout college by fully dressing the part of an entitled trust-fund child, garnering the attention of those seeking their MRS Degree.

Brian eventually became the CEO of a health insurance company. He was worth a fortune. His wife, Bethany, a woman so proper and neat she appeared sterile, had given birth to a baby girl just one month before Eli was born and six months before Brian McDonald heard his own name being uttered through the walls of a tent in a prophecy being given by Willow Breckburn, Old Willow, the Most Accurate Fortune-Teller in the World. Brian McDonald was not the sort to go to a fair and had only done so at the request of a colleague who hoped to lure McDonald into public service. The mogul's daughter, Flora, was in a front pack that Brian wore to bond with his child.

Overhearing this foretelling, the thought of the baby girl he carried on his chest being married repulsed him. He nearly threw up on her head as he listened in on the prophecy. He followed Eli's parents out of the fairgrounds to their apartment, his wife asking where he was going at the corner of every new block. He suddenly stopped, placing his hand out to halt his wife in her tracks as Eli's parents climbed the steps outside their flat. Brian McDonald looked around, memorizing the neighborhood.

His wife wanted to know what was happening and he did a horrible job of explaining how and why he wanted to dispose of a baby he didn't even know. Giving up, he hailed one of the dozens of taxis that had been circling the fairgrounds, and they went home.

Brian McDonald obsessed over Eli. Almost daily, he walked by the apartment Eli's parents had entered following the fair. After a couple of weeks of stalking and pacing while stewing over the prophecy he had overheard from Old Willow, Brian McDonald made a phone call. Brian had a great many contacts. It wasn't hard for him to get the building Eli's parents lived in condemned, despite it being only ten years old.

Eli's mother, Megan Moran, worked for a solar energy company. More than coincidentally, the company was burned to the ground in a wildfire that had broken out just blocks away in the parking lot of a fast-food diner. The winds just happened to be blowing in the direction of Green Day Solar and were uncharacteristically constant that day. Local Fire Chief Jim McMahon described it as "The worse possible conditions you could have if you're trying to contain the fire."

Fortunately for Eli's family, there were no injuries. The company had offices in Minnesota to which much of Eli's mother's team relocated. "At least we have family to fall back on," Megan Moran said in an interview with local news. "A lot of people, including some of my fellow workers, don't have that. So, we're starting a fundraising campaign among those of us who can contribute. My husband is helping us with our on-line campaign."

Eli's father, Mike Anderson, was a climate activist, organizer, and member of a coalition that also had offices in Minnesota. Eli's parents had family in Minnesota who offered them a place to stay while they transitioned from homelessness, a state Mike would never acknowledge as such since they were lucky enough to have family to fall back on.

Mike had been an artist for most of his life after discovering, as a little boy, that he could make his siblings notice him by drawing them. Most of the drawings showed any number of siblings chasing him with sometimes blunt, but often sharp, objects. He would give these drawings to his mother as daily "gifts," featuring her at the center of the composition, looking angelic, prepared to pass judgment on his assailants. He grew into quite the athlete after developing a high level of endurance from constantly running away. In fact, Mike Anderson became a marathon runner. His tan skin and flowing golden hair made him resemble the FTD florist logo as he ran through the streets of Southern California - a look that played just as well in Minnesota, the land of the Vikings. Even so, losing their home was difficult for the Moran-Anderson clan.

Chapter 2

Brian McDonald gloated as he read the news. His plan to separate Eli from his baby daughter Flora had worked. As he laughed to himself over his despicable plan and its ruthless execution, he heard a knock at his office door. Before he could tell his receptionist to turn away whomever it was who dared to bother him at such a personally joyous time, a man stepped into his office.

"Congratulations Brian," the man grinned as he extended a hand across Brian's absurdly large, glass desk. "Please allow me to introduce myself. I, too, am a man of wealth and taste." As he said this, he pulled a pen from his pocket, twirling it through his fingers like a drumstick. "Welcome to the organization," the man smiled, "Here is your complimentary gold pen, a gesture of my good faith, and a symbol of our undying union."

"Who are you?" Brian McDonald blurted as he inspected the pen.

"Tut-tut, it isn't proper to interrupt someone before they have fully introduced themselves," the man said, still smiling. "If you do it again, I will have to seize you now, instead of waiting. And while that might cause a little trouble with the arrogant CEO of this thing you call life, I will do it if you interrupt me again."

Brian McDonald was about to end his own life at that moment by doing precisely what he was told not to do, until he noticed that the man was now hovering a good six inches off the floor. He slowly and silently sat back down as he tried to understand just what was happening.

"Good," the man continued, "everything works itself out in time, I always say. And who am I, you ask with those frightened little human eyes of yours? Well, I'm going to tell you. And what's better is that I am going to give you a golden opportunity." At this, the man laughed for such a long time that it became horribly uncomfortable, even cringeworthy. "Okay, okay, I'm sorry. No, actually, I am not. In fact, I am never sorry. It goes against my very nature and I don't tolerate it in those I surround myself with." Suddenly, the man was standing directly behind Brian McDonald with one hand resting on his shoulder. "You see, Brian, I am Beelzebub, Satan, the Devil - whichever term you like - I am he."

Brian McDonald sat frozen in his chair, even though his shoulder was literally on fire. He was unable to speak.

"Oops," the devil snickered as he brushed the fire away from Brian's three-hundred-dollar shirt and spun Brian's chair around to face him. "Now, let's talk business."

"But I don't believe in hell, or heaven for that matter," Brian said as he regained his voice.

"Well, Brian baby, that part isn't really necessary. You see, it doesn't matter what you believe or don't believe - the simple fact of the matter is that I exist and so does my realm. And you, my little man, are just that, my little man."

"But..."

"Oh no, no, no, don't go spoiling your opportunity by interrupting me. You have no idea what I am prepared to offer you." The Devil leapt up into the air and floated down like a high jumper in slow motion. Before his body reached the floor, a long chaise lounge chair appeared beneath him, stopping his fall as he rested his head on a luxurious pillow. "I was truly impressed with that wildfire you had started the other day, purely out of spite, over a prophecy from a two-bit carny fortune-teller. That is pure Hell material there, m'boy." Filing his nails, the Devil continued, "I have great plans for you, Brian. I see a future where you cause massive suffering,

13

depression, and death. And the true beauty of it all is that you don't have to change a thing. You just do you."

Beelzebub jumped up once again and the lounge chair disappeared. "Y'know, Brian, I have seen your like before. Hell, the Catholic Church is my organization. In fact, I coopted the kid's legacy before they finished writing his story. Y'know, Jesus. He was never expected to blow up as big as he has, but that's an entirely different story. You see, you are a child of God and he is so disappointed in all of you that he gave me Earth a long time ago. But I digress, I am so confident that I know you so well that I am going to tell you a secret. Do you see these three golden hairs?" Satan ran his fingers through his own hair but didn't wait for an answer. "They are your ticket to freedom. You can go anywhere you like when you die if you possess even one of the three golden hairs of an angel. Even a fallen angel."

Satan leaned over Brian McDonald so closely that the three golden hairs were inches from his face. Impulsively, he grabbed for the hairs. Satan did not move. Brian had the hairs in his hand. Brian thought he had the hairs in his hand. Brian watched himself reaching for the hairs and taking them, only to have them disappear once again. Brian felt himself floating over the scene as it played over and over, always with the same result. Suddenly, sitting next to him, Brian felt Satan.

"I can take you any time I like."

Brian was sitting, sweating profusely and staring at his empty hand.

"However... I'd rather have you here Brian, where you can do me some good. And by that, I mean bad." Satan licked his finger. It sizzled as he did. He turned his finger to the air and placed it slightly above his head as if pressing on something. The air in front of his finger caught fire, leaving a fireball floating in Brian McDonald's office. "Now, that's how it's done," the Devil boasted. "You people get that gesture wrong every single time. The pathetic thing is you do it to make yourselves feel empowered. Possibly one of my favorite words right now. Empowered," Satan expounded, "is such a delicate word in this human climate, so dependent upon context, so prone to misuse."

"Like those women getting all worked up about equal pay for equal work. The men are the ones who have been doing all of the work. The women just barely got out the kitchen for Chrissake!" Brian said. He tried to hide behind his glass desk as he realized what he had just said and to whom he had said it.

"Exactly" exclaimed Beelzebub, grinning like the Devil. And he was gone.

Chapter 3

Brian didn't know if the Devil was gone or just lingering out of sight. But that afternoon, Brian returned to the fairgrounds. It was the very day Eli's family was moving out of their condemned flat. (A building, coincidentally, McDonald would later buy and reopen without a lick of work being done to it, passing inspection without a hitch. He was the consummate businessman.)

"You're here about the Devil thing, aren't you?" Old Willow said without looking up as Brian McDonald entered her tent slowly. "Sit down or go away," she said.

When Brian sat, Old Willow looked up. "You can put five hundred dollars, cash, right here on this table if you want me to keep talking."

McDonald started to speak.

"None of that 'I don't have it nonsense' either!" Old Willow pointed again to the table. "Remember who you're talkin' to. Hell, I don't need cards or a crystal ball for you. Hell, now that's funny. Apropos and funny." Old Willow sat silent.

"How do you know about the Devil?" Brian McDonald shouted above the sounds of a twenty-one-gun military salute to those in uniform, given by those who had served Orange County and the United States of America. The salute was fifteen guns shorter than McDonald expected, and he ended up yelling at Old Willow, who simply sat silent, chewing on beef jerky, while rolling a cigarette of American Spirit tobacco. "How do you know about the Devil and why should I pay you five hundred dollars? And don't joke about Hell, it's not a laughing matter. And, okay, dammit, here's the money." McDonald said as he peeled five, crisp, one-hundred-dollar bills from his billfold, placing them ceremoniously on the card table, then sat down on the folding chair.

"Do you want the good news or the bad news?" Old Willow asked dispassionately.

"Do I have a choice?" Brian responded.

"Of course you do, it's your money." The old fortune teller grinned.

"Then I will take the good news." McDonald responded.

"You are going to be President of the United States." Old Willow said to the astonishment of Brian McDonald, who fell silent as he thought about what being the president could do for business.

"Will I profit from being President?" he asked as he leaned in across the table, eager for information.

"Oh yes, you will gain extraordinary wealth, far beyond what you currently hold." Old Willow continued, "Your businesses will have exponential growth as your administration reshapes the global economy and landscape. Instigating and enacting policy that directly benefits you will be one of the defining characteristics of your administration."

Brian McDonald was elated. He jumped out of his chair, pacing with enthusiasm within the limited tent space. "I'm going to be rich!" He corrected himself, "I'm going to be richer!" He laughed himself to tears. Slowly, his sobbing turned from joyful to fearful. "Wait!" He straightened up and pointed a rigid finger at Old Willow. "You said do I want the good news or the bad news, so what's the bad news?"

Old Willow dropped her eyes to the table. "It's going to take five more of those for the bad news," she said as she pointed to the one-hundred-dollar bills.

"No way, I paid you fair and square. You said five hundred." McDonald argued.

"I gave you a choice. I specifically asked you, "Do you want the good news or the bad news?" And you said you wanted the good news. Now, if you wanted both, you should have said so and we could have made arrangements but, as it stands, you got what you asked for, and so a new arrangement must be agreed upon." She looked up at Brian McDonald and smiled, "So, for five hundred dollars, I will tell you the bad news."

"Screw you," Brian McDonald yelled as he stormed out of the tent.

Old Willow sat at her table and arranged the bills into five parallel columns, then turned her gaze toward the entrance to her tent.

Brian McDonald slowly re-entered the tent, a look of complete contempt and frustration upon his face, "Okay you old witch, I'll give you another five hundred for the bad news, but I want all of it!"

"I'm sorry Mr. McDonald, that deal is no longer on the table." Old Willow said softly, "but I would be happy to tell you "all of it" as you put it, for an additional one thousand dollars."

"What kind of racket are you running here, old lady?" McDonald complained, "I just left a minute ago; prices don't go up that fast for anything!"

"This from an insurance CEO, hilarious. Look mister, it's my tent, one thousand or bye-bye. See here," she said as she motioned to the table, "I've made it easy on you. Simply place two more of those lovely little hundred dollar bills you have in your billfold on each of these rows, and we have a deal."

Brian McDonald, reluctantly but firmly, laid down one thousand dollars, two hundred in each row, as he sat back down at the table. "There you go, Satisfied?" He growled across the table, "Now I want it all, everything, no holding back and nothing left out. I want the future, everything you can see, got me?"

"As you wish, Mr. McDonald," Old Willow laid one row upon the other until all the bills were in a single stack. She grabbed the whole stack, turned around in her seat and lifted the lid from a cookie jar on the top shelf of an old cabinet, wedged into the corner of the tent. "You want to know what the Devil is up to, don't you Mr. McDonald?" she asked as she placed the cash in the jar.

"I assume that's the bad news," McDonald said fearfully.

"You are absolutely right, Mr. McDonald, that is the bad news," Willow Breckburn said with the hint of a smile on her lips. "In a nutshell," she leaned in closer and whispered over the table, her breath a mixture of beef jerky and cigarettes, "you are a subject of the almighty ruler of the underworld, Satan's little toy, for eternity."

"What in God's name does that mean?" McDonald snapped.

"Interesting choice of words," Old Willow snickered, "But you're not wrong. I could spend days talking about that, but I'm sure it would bore you, because it isn't just about you. So, let's get down to the nitty gritty. Did he show you the hairs? Y'know, the three golden hairs?"

Brian McDonald sat bolt upright, "How did you..."

"Never mind, any one of us worth our salt know about the three golden hairs of an angel. Betcha couldn't grab 'em could ya? Of course you couldn't - maybe he didn't even let you try. That's stupid. Of course he did. Probably got a good laugh out of it too. I mean, he is the Devil after all. Most, if not all, of his joy comes in taunting, ridiculing and otherwise menacing mankind by allowing people to dig their own graves, so to speak." Old Willow reached into her pocket and pulled out a peanut. She carefully opened the shell and removed one of two nuts inside, which she ate. "Nut?" she said as she held the half-shell out to Brian McDonald.

"No, forget the nut, how do I get the hairs?" Brian McDonald was quite sure that he hated Old Willow.

"You can't," Old Willow continued, "ain't gonna happen. There is no way you will ever be able to remove any hairs from the head of Satan, especially the golden ones. There is no record, or even a rumor, of any angel ever being bribed, forced or tricked into giving up their golden hairs." She added, "There are stories of individuals who have tried to steal the golden hairs of an angel, but those have all ended miserably. So, more bad news - you actually tried to take them from Satan, which, according to all tales, told and untold, means that you are going to end up in permanent service to the Devil."

"I can't accept that," McDonald cried, "I won't accept that! I paid you plenty. You haven't told me the whole truth. You're keeping something from me, I know it." Brian McDonald rose from his chair and glared menacingly down at the old woman. "I told you what the deal was, I want to know what is going to happen in the future, my future, all of it! There has to be some way to get those hairs, now tell me or you're going to wish I never came in here!"

Old Willow stared wistfully off into space. "I have heard of one case where a human came to be in possession of the three golden hairs of an angel, but the same could never happen to you."

McDonald reached behind his back, pulled a handgun from his belt and sat down, pointing the gun directly in Old Willow's face. "Tell me how that happened, or I am going to pull this trigger."

"Just put the gun away, Mr. McDonald. You're wasting the effort on me. I've lived a full life and have no fear of death." Willow Breckburn sighed deeply, "I will tell you what I know, all of it. It ain't gonna save you." Old Willow brought both hands up high in the air and watched McDonald's eyes follow. "You are going to be rich beyond belief. President of the United States, the most powerful man in the world." She wiggled her fingers like confetti dancing in zero gravity. "You will be surrounded by wealth, power and beauty." Old Willow nearly broke her own card table as she brought her hands down with a deafening slap. "And then you will die!" Her eyes directly across from his, she told Brian, "Unless you have one of the three golden hairs of an angel, you will serve Satan for eternity."

"I'm gonna need all of those golden hairs - they must be worth a fortune." Brian McDonald put the gun back in his belt. He scowled; his tiny nose popped up closer to his angry eyes. "I need those three golden hairs. You. You said that a human got the three golden hairs before. You said you would tell me everything. Tell me how that human got the three golden hairs."

"There are only two ways to get the three golden hairs of an angel." Old Willow glared intently at Brian. "You take them, which you can't do because you are not immortal. Or you are given them, which is more than unlikely in your case. Well, in anyone's case, really, since there are only a few known instances in all of humankind's existence where a mortal was gifted the three golden hairs by an immortal. The most recent, of course, being Liberace, which only makes sense, given the en caul birth." Old Willow stood up, "Okay, that's it. The truth, the whole truth and nothing but the truth, so help me Jesus. And now it's time for you to leave."

McDonald stood up but did not leave. "Hold on, what was all that stuff about on call birth and Liberace?"

"En caul, Mr. McDonald, e-n c-a-u-l. Google it." She motioned toward the exit, "Now, please."

It was clear by the look on her face that any more questions would not be answered. Brian McDonald had already threatened death and, though ruthless, was incapable of torture. He had already subconsciously thanked himself for not blowing the old lady's head off because he was quite sure that he would vomit and more than likely pass out at the sight of it, ensuring his capture as a murderer. So he left.

Chapter 4

Seventeen years later, all was as Old Willow had predicted. President Brian McDonald was enriching himself daily, making deals to stuff his pockets while gutting programs to help the people. He had become the ultimate corporate president, adored by the rich and entitled.

Eli grew up in a loving household and was truly a lucky child. One might argue that their family's displacement was, in fact, a blessing rather than a curse. It provided an opportunity that enabled their family of three to thrive. They might not sum things up in the same way because they viewed the world as their home and climate change was still being accelerated by a species Eli rarely felt a part of. They learned a lot about the climate from their parents and decided to create a YouTube channel devoted to the issue of climate change. Eli's popularity grew as they spoke out against a system that was controlled by an elite class whose only interest was profits. People of all ages followed the channel that Eli created when they were a freshman in high school.

Eli was nearly a senior when it happened. Flora McDonald fell madly in love with a YouTube celebrity.

She was looking for sources for a social studies presentation when she first discovered Eli. There was something about them that immediately captivated Flora. They had a confidence and a matter-of-factness that Flora rarely found in her own social circle. In fact, the only person who exhibited these same traits as strongly as Eli was Flora's own father. She was now the daughter of a dad she loved and a president she hated. He spent time with her. He talked to his daughter and listened to her when she agreed with him and when she didn't. He let her just be a person, unlike her mother and the media. However, Flora binge-watched Eli's YouTube channel daily until she was totally caught up on them, and that changed everything. She began to think about how different the public person was from the person she knew as her father. She wondered how he could be so caring and concerned about her but not about everyone else.

Flora McDonald had become something of a household name after an argument she had with her father was caught on video and went viral. Her point, though valid, was unsupported by critical data. She had built her case entirely on what she learned from Eli's podcast and memes and did a terrible job of assembling her thoughts into a defensible narrative. Her father was a great debater. He loved to hear himself talk. He would talk over people and they would let him. He basically trounced his daughter for telling him that plastic straws were harmful to the environment. To add insult to injury, he asked for extra straws when his beer came, a beverage he didn't normally use straws to drink.

Eli saw the video. They wondered what it must be like to have such a monster for a father. Their father was a caring climate activist. Their mother was also working to save the Earth that they would inherit, so long as Flora's father didn't blow it up. Certainly, there must be something they could do to help Flora. They didn't have the clout or the capital to spread the word like the mass media did, but Eli was going to send a message to more than five hundred thousand viewers that they were on Flora's side. Eli built a much stronger case against the overuse of plastics while calling out corporate negligence and greed. They backed up Flora, then added that what she was facing was what an entire nation was facing. Society had become consumptive to the point of blindness. Eli closed the broadcast with a personal message to Flora reminding her that "we are all in this together."

Two things happened then that day. Flora and Brian McDonald, each, from officers in two different security agencies, requested information on Eli. The only thing either of them knew about them was that they had a YouTube channel called "Awesome Things from the Past" because today is tomorrow's past. Flora knew the why part of it all, but her father only knew that they had become viral by "sticking their nose into a personal and private family conversation." He chose to ignore the fact that Eli was commenting on a video that had already gone viral.

Lieutenant Julie Maxwell had become something of a hero to Flora. The day they met, Julie was the only person on the White House staff to speak to Flora like an adult. Everyone else kept pointing out things Flora didn't care about, like which bedroom in the White House had belonged to whom. She was quick to admit that she sucked at History. She was just beginning to understand the relationship of history to the issues Eli was not only exposing but explaining in a way that kept her interest more than school ever had. Julie was someone Flora felt she could talk to, and she did. Eli had come up often by the time the infamous "Straw Video" appeared.

Lieutenant Maxwell found Eli first and brought them to the White House that same day. Quietly, and with their permission, as well as the permission of their parents. The President was not notified. The First Lady was away for some alone time, with a television crew, in the Bahamas. She was not there to aid the residents after climate change had ravaged their island. She was not planning to visit Puerto Rico because she didn't realize it was part of the United States. Even if she had, she would not care or even pretend to think that she could do anything about it because she believed these things happen in nature all the time and the danger from climate change is greatly exaggerated. When asked by the TV crew, many of whom were locals hired to help lug around all the equipment necessary to "document" her travels, if she believed in climate change, she responded, "Of course, there's climate change. It wouldn't be any fun if it was always the same!"

Julie had texted Flora immediately when she knew Eli was willing to drop everything and fly to the White House. The effects of the helicopter on the environment had been immediately mentioned by the Moran-Anderson family who received the obvious response, "Well, we're already here, so you may as well get in the helicopter." Mike Anderson was going to counter with an argument that bringing them back would double the emissions but worried that his intentions may be misunderstood and that he might never see home again. Also, Eli had already run to the chopper.

Mike Anderson ducked his head as he approached the aircraft and saluted everyone he encountered. He even saluted the back of the head of the pilot. He did the same all the way through the White House, even though he had never served in the military. His long blonde hair had turned white shortly after he reached the age of fifty. Eli had seen the change as an opportunity to make a statement, using their father's head as the canvas. They painstakingly separated his ponytail into seven distinct strands which they colored blue, green, yellow, orange, red and purple, leaving one strand white. Then, they wove the strands into a rainbow ponytail. They continued the practice ever since. Today, Mike was sporting a freshly dyed rainbow.

Eli had been in full stride since they disembarked the helicopter with a leap. They seemed to know the White House like they seemed to know a lot of things. Eli felt at ease under the watch of Lieutenant Maxwell, who was noticeably liked by the White House staff. They navigated the halls as if drawn by magnetic forces. Eli looked back to make sure their father was still with them. They imagined their father separated from them without Lieutenant Maxwell to explain his presence in the White House. Fortunately, he was close behind as moving briskly to keep up was no issue for him. Eli stopped and stood staring, captivated by their father's ponytail fluttering a rainbow upon the sea of red, white and blue flags that lined the hallways. They thought about pulling out their phone to capture the moment on video but held up when they noticed Lieutenant Maxwell, single-handed, perfectly panning through the shot Eli saw in their mind.

"That's one hell of a ponytail," Julie laughed as she touched her screen to end the shot. "Okay now, Flora's waiting and I gotta get back up front before, well, you know who." Lieutenant Maxwell pocketed her phone and shut her mouth. They had reached the Blue Room.

Flora was sitting when Eli arrived. She was extremely nervous until she saw them. She jumped up out of the chair and ran to Eli. "You're here! You came to my house!"

"Like I had a choice," Eli laughed as they pointed over their shoulder with their thumb. "Who can resist a bad-ass black woman in uniform who arrives in a jet-black helicopter, packing heat?"

Flora hadn't visualized what would happen on Eli's end of things when she reached out to Julie, but she knew no matter what, that Julie would handle it properly. She knew her father well enough to suspect that he was going to go after Eli. What she didn't know was that Julie made it to Eli only moments before a full-scale military SWAT operation surrounded the Moran-Anderson home in South Minneapolis.

"They're gone already," Megan Moran smiled as she sat on her front steps. She waved a piece of paper over her head, both of her hands in the air. "Lieutenant Maxwell said you'd want to see this" she added. An officer, who had arrived in a jet-black Hummer, only a minute before, spoke into a handset and two hovering helicopters flew off in unison.

"Thank you, ma'am," the officer responded as he took the paper. He opened it, looked at the paper for a moment and continued, "we are truly sorry for interrupting you ma'am and hope you have a pleasant day." The officer turned back to his vehicle, raised his hand over his head and made a large circle in the air. The other soldiers returned to their vehicles and drove off. A collection of neighbors slowly emerged from their homes to watch the vehicles drive away. Some looked to the sky to see if they could see the helicopters. Many looked at Megan and walked slowly toward her, attempting to achieve the right pace between nosiness and caring.

An elderly woman, with a dog no bigger than a squirrel, called from across the street, "Everything okay dear?"

"Oh yeah, fine, Harriet, y'know, just another fan of Eli's!" Megan stood up, brushed off her hiking shorts and headed toward the path along the river for her daily walk.

Eli received attention wherever they went. People were drawn to them. Eli was comfortable and familiar to everyone. It was hard to watch them and dislike them, even if you disagreed with their politics, taste or atheism. When confronted, as a thirteen-year-old child, about their atheism by a minister who was recruiting for a climate activist organization, they summed up their position as just that, one side of a topic for debate. "I don't believe God exists. I don't care that you do. As far as I'm concerned, the burden of proof is on your side." Eli flashed their smile, the one that made everyone immediately want to be around them. "Now, sign me up and show me what I can do to help."

Just like the minister became quick friends with Eli, so did the White House staff. Several members of the White House staff were called in to the Blue Room to ensure that word didn't spread to the President. All were quite sure they had met Eli before or recognized them as a previous guest, when in fact, Eli had never met any of them before and had never been to the White House. They all swore to not tell the President until Flora was ready to let him know that Eli had been located.

Colonel Sanders, and, yes, he gets that all the time, was the officer the President had called into the Oval Office regarding Eli. Colonel Sanders had owed Lieutenant Maxwell a favor, the kind a more nefarious subordinate might lord over her superior officer. Julie used it to help Flora. Sanders delayed his report. He popped his head into the Blue Room to let Maxwell know but was quickly asked in by Flora. She wanted him to meet Eli. After talking to Eli for fifteen minutes, Colonel Sanders left the room laughing, "I still owe you one, Maxwell, this one's on me."

"Wow! How do you do that?" Flora exclaimed as she practically fell into Eli. "I mean, never mind," she laughed as she realized she knew exactly how they did it.

"I was going to ask you the same thing." Eli smiled an "I get you" smile. "How did you get the courage to bring up plastic straws to your father?"

Flora starting crying. It was the cry that happened eighty-three percent of the time once the "I get you" smile had been flashed. Most people who had seen it would spill their guts to Eli without fear about any number of subjects and Eli made them feel heard. She wiped her eyes, "Finally!" Flora spun around, holding both sides of her head, pulling her hair out, wincing through her teeth, "I thought I was going crazy. Everybody acted like I was supposed to be a scientist with all the facts. I had a hard-enough time just bringing the whole thing up. I mean, I know my dad. He doesn't want anybody to stop making stuff."

"And look, you got the whole world talking about consumption now." Eli strode toward an ornate blue and gold chair, inspected it, turned around and sat in it and said, "Everything is rush, rush, rush, hurry, hurry, hurry, no quality, just speed, mass production, mass consumption. Unlike this amazing chair I am sitting in, with its fine gold accents, and so comfortable." Eli motioned toward the other chair and Flora sat.

Lieutenant Maxwell began walking toward the door, "You know where to find me, Flora." Julie Maxwell waited until the other staff members left the room. "Your father is still in the hallway, talking to my pilot. I'm going to ask him to join me in my office until you're ready, Eli."

"Thank you, Lieutenant." Eli added, "but be careful, he's likely to go on a rant about the effect the Military Industrial Complex continues to have on climate change."

"You're amazing, Eli," Flora said as Maxwell left the room. "You just talk to everyone. You say exactly what you want but somehow manage to get everyone to like you, even if it isn't what they want to hear. I hate to say this, but you have got to meet my father."

At that moment, the President of the United States entered the room. He walked directly to Eli, who stood immediately upon seeing the President enter the room. "Brian McDonald," the President said, "but you can call me Mr. President, or sir." McDonald laughed as he patted Eli on the shoulder. "Just kidding, just kidding, you can call me Brian," He smiled over Eli, "of course, that is if you let me call you Eli. Deal?" He extended a hand to Eli who shook it firmly.

"It would be a privilege, Sir Brian!" Eli saluted the President and stood at attention.

President McDonald burst out laughing. He had fully intended to dislike Eli. He had never watched Eli's video all the way through. Eli's first criticism of the President was twelve seconds in, and McDonald tuned out by the half-minute mark. Meeting Eli was a different story entirely, they controlled the energy of the room wherever they went. Brian McDonald became uncomfortable though outwardly gregarious. He pulled a blue chair from in front of the fireplace and positioned it next to his daughter's. He sat down. Eli and Flora immediately followed suit.

"Dad?" Flora asked as she sat, an awkward, guilty smile on what she described as her desperately average face, "How did you know we were here?"

"The cameras, my dear." He smiled and watched his daughter's face transfigure into an expression that was far from average, as she imagined him watching her. "Don't look so distressed, Flora. I wasn't watching you." That was a lie.

The meeting continued awkwardly as the President did his best to assure his daughter that he had only her best interest at heart while attempting to trick Eli into saying something that would upset Flora. Instead, Brian McDonald succeeded in further illuminating the gap between most of the people in his generation and hers. His assumption that everyone in America believed it was the country's right to determine policy in other nations under the banner of "Democracy" was shattered when Flora said, "But Daddy, you're the President of the United States of America, not Bolivia, Venezuela, Afghanistan, Ukraine or anywhere else for that matter. Don't you have enough to worry about here?"

He had expected an argument like that to come from Eli, not his own daughter. "It's more complicated than that." Brian McDonald stood up and brushed himself off, as if that very action could sweep away the uneasy feeling in his gut. He had no clue what was really going on in the world and relied heavily on what he was told by his generals.

"Why?" Flora and Eli asked in unison.

"It's adult stuff," McDonald responded dismissively as he retreated from the Blue Room.

Julie Maxwell was good to her word and returned Eli and their father back home after Flora had what she would later call the most wonderful, eye-opening and mind-blowing afternoon of her life. No one in their right mind could call her face average, unless average now meant radiating the light of possibility. In fact, the whole notion, that any face could be average, was no longer in her mind, after spending the afternoon with Eli. They had made her feel special in a way that no one else ever had, not even her father.

Lieutenant Maxwell helped Flora meet with Eli a half-dozen times over the following year without the President being aware. He had put Eli behind him. His monitoring of his daughter's phone calls and her behavior on social media was thorough. Flora became aware of the activity when her father instructed her to change all her social media accounts in accordance with a "suggestion" from the Department of Homeland Security. Fortunately, she and Eli had agreed to avoid any means of communication that could be easily traced. No one thought to see if she had mastered the ancient art of letter-writing. Her social media profile wasn't even her own. It was managed by a team at the White House and read like a series of press releases. She quickly realized what her father was up to when a long string of teen boys materialized at White House functions where, previously, there had been none. She had no interest in any of them.

Her meetings with Eli were not only secret but exhilarating.

Chapter 5

Flora graduated from a private high school three days after Eli graduated from public high school. Both graduated with honors. Eli was valedictorian, an achievement that was celebrated by their entire class. The valedictorian at Flora's school was largely ignored in the shadow of Flora's graduation party, the plan for which made national news and bloated social media with accolades and insults.

Flora wanted only one thing for graduation - Eli at her party. She never talked to her father about Eli, a policy that may have saved their life. Instead, Brian McDonald was blissfully ignorant that Flora was not only communicating with Eli but deeply in love with them. That bliss was shattered when Eli arrived at Flora's party in a car they had built with their parents. It was really six or seven cars Frankensteined together with a solar panel array. It was entirely electric and charged completely by solar power. Lieutenant Maxwell had cleared Eli for entrance to the grounds of the White House. People swarmed the vehicle as it pulled up, some to look at the car, others to get a closer look at Eli, whose subscribers had just passed the million mark. Flora was fastidiously greeting the various dignitaries invited by her father, when the son of Japan's Prime Minister excused himself for impulsively diverting his attention from her. He recognized Eli, who, smiling and silent, had stepped alongside Flora. Flora became slightly uncomfortable until Eli bowed, exchanged a brief handshake and greeted the son of the Prime Minister in Japanese.

President Brian McDonald was deep in conversation with a Saudi Arabian prince when Eli arrived. He had intended to introduce the prince to Flora until he saw the exchanges between Eli and the row of dignitaries they were now greeting in unison with his daughter. Despite his rage over Eli's presence at Flora's party, McDonald controlled himself. He was pragmatic. He recognized that Eli had played the moment perfectly, without knowing and without effort. Old Willow's prophecy appeared to be manifesting before his eyes. Brian McDonald thought of a plan and he thought it up quick.

"Excuse me," the President announced as he moved to his daughter, gently turning her shoulder from the line of dignitaries still waiting to extend their best wishes on her graduation. "I apologize," he motioned toward the line, "we appreciate all of you who have come so far to honor our family with your presence. If I may take a moment." McDonald was no fool. He immediately assessed that his daughter and Eli had been meeting without his knowledge. He also realized that this was not the moment to expose that fact and instead feigned ignorance. "Isn't that the kid from online," he asked Flora quietly, "the one with the video about the straws?" Brian McDonald was seething inside. His forced smile looked like that of a child who had just bitten into a chocolate covered caramel only to discover it was, in fact, filled with maple flavored nougat.

Flora could sense her father's anger but leveraged the setting to keep Eli safe. She was an excellent student who had been accepted to Boston Institute of Technology's engineering program after her mother had hired a college placement firm to assist Flora in her search for the finest engineering schools in the country. "I'd like to take a moment to make an announcement, since so many of you have kindly gathered here to show your support. Eli and I are going to be roommates at BIT in September!"

The crowd burst into applause as President McDonald swallowed the maple nugget of truth. His daughter had grown up and was becoming her own person, despite his best efforts to control her. A further realization slowly sunk in as he glad-handed the throngs of congratulants. Flora had applied to and been accepted by BIT, elected to live on-campus and, presumably, used her influence as the First Daughter to choose her roommate. The last of these events did not actually occur. Eli and Flora were assigned to the same room because they were the first freshmen to elect to live on campus, because they were the first freshmen to be accepted. Both were offered scholarships, and both donated them to the students who had the lowest income according to the FAFSA, a notion Eli had suggested to all whose families could afford full tuition on their own, during their most shared episode on their YouTube channel.

An intense debate had broken out in many households and across all media, as a result of the episode. A debate Brian McDonald would have joined, if he hadn't finally agreed to the First Lady's relentless requests to take a few days away from it all, causing him to miss it entirely. To those who spoke with him about the issue, he appeared wise and patient, when in fact he was oblivious and evasive. The President only became aware of the truth after it was discussed at length by those assembled at the party. President Brian McDonald had become the consummate actor.

Bethany McDonald was the ultimate first lady, at least publicly, in a Nancy Reagan fashion. She supported her husband, entertained visitors to the White House, joined societies and attended gala events with and without her husband. Her relationship with Flora was adversarial for most of her daughter's childhood but became almost non-existent after Brian was elected to the office of president. She had once adored her husband but since Flora's birth became intensely jealous of his love for their daughter. She shut herself off from both and retreated into fashion and travel. Had

Bethany been brighter, she might have enjoyed the conversations Brian and Flora shared.

Bethany spent Flora's entire lifetime competing for attention with her. Brian only focused on Flora. Bethany and Brian only argued when it came to Flora. Before Flora was in the picture, both were mutually self-absorbed and just as mutually pleased to be doing it together. Had Bethany been any brighter, she would have easily been able to recognize that Flora had help from Lieutenant Maxwell in arranging secret meetings with Eli. However, her fascination with her own beauty and possessions blinded her to the obvious. Had she been more observant she would most certainly have been able to rebut her husband's accusations that evening, after the graduation party.

"You're the one who let that Eli kid in here," the President paced across the floor of their spacious White House bedroom. "This is all because I wouldn't let you have Deepak Chopra over here for a retreat with thirty of your closest friends. I've already told you a million times, the White House isn't a spa. It's bad enough you turned one of the banquet halls into your own personal fitness room. You used to go on and on about what a great example Michelle Obama was for young women, but the moment I win the election, her stuff isn't good enough for you."
Bethany McDonald was always a bit of a deer in the headlights when her husband would yell at her before the election. Many times, she had considered leaving Brian, late nights after he had been out meeting other high-powered businessmen, early mornings when he would walk in smelling of perfume only to complain that some other guy had brought his wife along to stink up the meeting. But Brian had always given her everything she asked for and that

made it difficult to leave him. No president had ever experienced a divorce while in office and that fact gave Bethany her voice.

"Can it, Brian!" Bethany McDonald replied, barely looking up from her magazine as she all but ignored the President. "Today was the first time I have seen Flora in the past three weeks. I'm working on myself here, Brian. I don't have time to help the two of you through your little quarrels. Oh, and by the way, those roses you sent me to cover your guilt for sleeping with that intern of yours, didn't cut it. I couldn't care less about your transgressions. They just make the settlement I'll be getting at the end of your term more appealing, but those roses weren't even sustainably raised, so I sent them back."

Since the trip to the Bahamas, Bethany McDonald had discovered Oprah. She had always heard of her but didn't watch her because she was black. Bethany had had enough of Brian at the graduation party and switched-on Oprah to clear her mind. "What's this? Look, Brian, Oprah is in our bedroom."

The bed the McDonalds shared could have slept a family of twelve. "Oprah really gets around," Brian turned out the lights and climbed into his side of the bed. Bethany clapped and the TV turned off. She stared at the ceiling and thought about Oprah and roses. The glow from the bedside lamp next to Bethany didn't even reach Brian's side of the bed as he closed his eyes and tried to clear his mind of Old Willow's prophecy.

That night, Brian dreamed of the Devil. He saw the Devil sleeping, his head in the lap of an old woman. In his dream, Brian also saw Eli. They were standing in the center of an elevator. Just as the elevator door closed, Brian noticed something in Eli's hand, three small, brilliant, golden hairs.

.

Chapter 6

Brian McDonald did not, however, change anything he did as President. He never bothered to separate himself from his business holdings while holding office. In fact, in direct conflict with the foreign Emoluments clause in the Constitution, he maintained his position as CEO of the largest insurance provider in the country, while becoming the CEO and principal shareholder of the largest oil company in the United States. He then used the military to overthrow the government of the sovereign nation of Venezuela, putting in power a puppet president, groomed and educated in the United States. He then made a deal with that government to get the oil, a natural resource previously controlled by the true government of Venezuela and her people.

Congress could not pull together enough support to win in a lawsuit they brought against President McDonald. "Our conclusion is straightforward because 28 Senators and 184 Members of the House of Representatives -- do not constitute a majority of either body and are, therefore, powerless to approve or deny the President's acceptance of foreign emoluments," the court said.

McDonald brazenly waved the headlines in front of the press, gathered around Air Force One, hoping for another soundbite from the leader of the corporate world takeover. He obliged. "Once again, the majority is with me, because America is great again. We will never give up the right to do business with anyone we want, whenever we want. God Bless America!" For a fleeting moment, Brian McDonald thought twice about what he had said. He had never used the "God Bless America" line in his entire presidency, until now. He feared another visit from the Devil more than anything else in the world and worried that he might upset the Devil, when in fact, the opposite was true.

"God Bless America indeed," the Devil cooed as he stroked Jesus, his favorite cat. "You know, Jesus, it's a pity that more people can't see the real me." Jesus settled into the Devil's lap and purred. "Oh yes, of course, you're right again, Jesus. Most of them ARE the real me. Sometimes I forget how clever you really are." Jesus yawned.

The media barely acknowledged that a sitting president was profiting from his position and focused instead on the boost in the stock market as the result of American interests around the globe. They applauded McDonald for his compassion when he added candy and soft drinks to "boost the spirit" of the refugee children held in cages at the southern border, a result of the various coups initiated, and sanctions imposed by the blessed nation.

Things got even better for Brian when he bombed Syria. The media cheered him on as he unleashed an attack on a nation with whom the United States was not at war, claiming that her leader had gassed his own people. Rational people, most of whom did not make their living by regurgitating lies of the state, were able to see through the deception. ISIS had finally been defeated in Syria, and trade agreements, beneficial to its people and its leaders, were imminent. There was no way anyone should have believed what United States intelligence agencies were claiming was happening in Syria. Assad would not have been gassing his own people – clearly not after his administration had tried so hard to put the country on a road to recovery after it was torn apart by radicals spurred on by outside forces. Still, Americans continued to accept that people trying to live in their own countries were somehow, in the words of mass-media, "a threat to our young men and women in uniform." These talking heads were referring to the American soldiers who had moved in and constructed bases the size of entire cities within countries in which they were not welcome.

McDonald was riding high on a wave of media support unlike any he had seen in his presidency. This enthusiasm was not reflected by Flora, who would not open the door for him when he visited her penthouse in Boston. Brian spoke to her in a voice he only used with her, a voice that had nauseated her ever since she was fifteen. At first, she didn't have the heart to tell him and although she had made it resoundingly clear since she had moved out of the White House, Brian still spoke to her as though she were six years old. "Flora, honey, I brought you something."

Flora watched her father through the lens in her door as he fumbled through his pockets for anything of interest. He found several candy wrappers and a mint toothpick. He landed on his billfold and peeled off twenty crisp, hundred-dollar bills, "it's money," he sang to the door.

"I don't need any more of your money, Dad," she said, feeling even further away from him than when he arrived. She watched as he motioned to Morty to find something in his pockets. Morton Fedelstein hurriedly patted himself down, trying to find anything Flora might like, but came up short. He quickly implored the two secret service agents to look as well. Nothing. The elevator door opened and a young woman with dark skin stepped out with a cleaning cart.

Brian McDonald instantly knew what to do. "Honey, if you open the door, I will give this money to the nice young lady who is out here with us now. She's a poor cleaning lady who has nothing and you can help her." The poor cleaning lady smiled a fake smile at the President and parked her cart outside the door of the adjacent penthouse.

Flora didn't want the woman to miss out but could clearly see that she was not going to belittle herself by getting into the middle of the President's infantile negotiations. The woman knocked three times on the door at the other end of the hallway and was preparing to let herself in when Flora opened her door. She looked right past her father as she snatched the bills from his hand. "Excuse me Rosalita," Flora smiled as she walked to meet Rosalita in the hallway. "Take this, please. And thank you for all your hard work."

Rosalita returned the smile and accepted the cash. She looked toward the President and said, "I didn't vote for you," then returned to her work.

"Well, a lot of people did," Brian said quietly as he stepped briskly into Flora's apartment, "didn't they Fiddlyhopper?" Morton Fedelstein was nothing if not loyal.

"Quite a number of people did, in fact, vote for you, sir." Fedelstein practically hopped into the apartment after the President looked his way then pointed to a spot twelve inches in front of his own feet, because Morton Fedelstein was nothing if not obedient.

"You know Fetalpop," the President stared intently into Morton's eyes, "I'm going to need something to eat." Flora had just walked past him when he became louder, "and so is Flora." The President laid his hand on Fedelstein's back and moved him like he was sliding a pint glass across a bar, toward Flora. "Ask Flora what she wants to eat."

Morty was awkward around most people but especially around female people. He wanted to play it cool. He wanted to be casual but respectful. He began the way he began with everyone, "Hello, I'm Morty, he, him, his," then he extended his hand.

"That's hilarious!" Flora smiled and gave Morty a hug, "You act like we just met." It was true that Flora and Morty had known each other since the morning after the graduation. Morty just never felt as though they had been formally introduced, which was also not entirely true. It was more that Morty had never actually been in a situation with Flora where he had to speak to her. Now he was in a situation where he needed to get a response as well. Flora had become a real people person since moving out of the White House. She and Eli would sit for hours, watching people and imagining their lives. She imagined that Morty was beyond nervous. "Fish and Chips, Morty, tartar sauce, malt vinegar, ketchup, the whole shebang. Dad loves fish and Chips, Morty. You can never go wrong with fish and chips and my dear old Dad."

Brian could feel the sarcasm but Morty was happy to have an answer and made for the door. "And coleslaw, plenty of coleslaw," the President shouted as Morty slammed the door in his haste to be diligent.

"Hey Bill, hey Amy," Flora greeted the secret service agents as she motioned to the empty chairs behind them. They stepped slowly and evenly backwards toward opposite corners of the room, checking the windows on their way. "Suit yourselves, it's going to be awhile." The agents came to a stop in the opposing corners of the room. They did not sit. Their expressions mirrored one another despite their difference in height.

Flora first met Amy two days after moving into the White House. Flora had decided that the White House lawn would make a great disc golf course. She bought six pole-holes and set them up around the yard. On her first throw, the disc caught a little wind and ended up in a tree beside the house. As she puzzled over how she might retrieve the disc from such an unclimbable tree, she heard a voice pass above her.

"I can get that," Amy said as she reached well up into the branches.

Flora had never seen a seven-foot-two-inch woman before. She stood transfixed. Officer Amy Nicholson was dressed in an impeccable black suit, wore sunglasses and had her hair in a bun. She was Emma Peel on steroids. And now, she was holding a bright white, one-hundred-seventy-two-gram Sidewinder. "Do you play?" Flora asked.

"What do you mean?" Amy replied, "Do I ever play, or do I play this particular game?"

"Well, both, either, I don't know." Flora said, slightly flustered.

"Okay then, both." Amy placed the disc on her forefinger of her left hand and moving her hand slightly, began twirling the disc in a clockwise direction. "I'm not officially clocked in yet, so I suppose it's okay to toss a few holes. Mind if I join you?" She did not look at her hand as the disc continued to rotate. Behind her sunglasses, her eyes surveyed the position of the holes. Her head remained still. "Which one?"

Flora hadn't really thought about the order of the holes. She had intended to get one in, then go from there. But she was curious to see what Amy was capable of, so she pointed to the pole-hole that was furthest away. She had placed it on the other side of a row of trees, nearly out of sight. "That one," she challenged.

To call it lucky would have been forgivable, but Flora knew it wasn't. The disc hit the chains with the force of a small rocket. The flight path had been calculated and flawlessly realized. Flora jumped up and down with excitement at what was, by rough estimate, a five-hundred-foot hole-in-one.

"Now we're going to have to go get it," Amy said like she had just discovered a nail in her tire.

The next half-hour produced four out of five holes-in-one. The only hole that required more throws was the one Amy suggested Flora try first. To be fair, Flora did make the basket in two throws. No small achievement on a hole that was easily over three hundred feet and was also partially obscured.

Amy and Flora had become as good of friends as a secret service agent and the daughter of a president could be. Amy was always careful to visit with Flora in her civilian clothes after that first afternoon. The President became very fond of Amy and was certain to have her by his side whenever possible. He nicknamed her Kareem Abdul-Jabbar because he also was seven-foot-two inches tall. Flora didn't get the reference, but Amy did and felt greatly complimented by it. Amy was not the least bit political but was something of an encyclopedia of sports knowledge. She loved Flora and respected Brian's office and was willing to die for both.

Officer Bill Redford was quiet and solid. It was as if he had been created in a lab to be a secret service officer. What he lacked in height, which wasn't much at six-foot-three, he made up for in bulk. He was muscular, very muscular. His neck was the width of the President's thigh. It was as though three humans could stand together in the same amount of space he needed to stand alone. The President called him "Redwood."

So, Redwood and Kareem Abdul-Jabbar looked on as the President tried to find the words to speak to his daughter. His eyes would roll up to the ceiling, swim back and forth like slowly circling sharks, then dive to the floor as he shut his eyes and pursed his lips, making his tiny nose nearly disappear. Then he would gasp, throwing his head back and the cycle would begin again.

"Dad!" Flora snapped.

Nothing.

"Brian McDonald," she snapped again.

"Mr. President," she snapped a third time, "get a hold of yourself."

Still nothing.

"C'mon Daddy, tell me why you came here."

The President relaxed into his seat more and his eyes landed on those of his daughter. "See, you called me Daddy," he tilted his head in a way that all of America had come to know meant that he was very pleased with himself because he was getting his way, "wasn't so hard, was it?"

"Oh, for god's sake Daddy," Flora exhaled, "what do you want?"

"I thought you and your little socialist friends didn't believe in God." Brian McDonald could not control his urge to taunt Flora over Eli, despite his own plan to ingratiate himself upon them.

"Daddy!"

"Sorry," the President responded quickly even though, in his heart, he wasn't, "I'm just joking around. Really, I know you are going to think this sounds weird, but I had a dream about Eli."

At that moment, Eli let themselves into the apartment using their keycard. Amy was positioned so that she could see them at the slightest opening of the door. She lowered her hand from her weapon when she recognized Eli and smiled at them broadly.

"Eli," Flora beamed, "my father was just telling me that he had a dream about you."

"Mr. President," Eli greeted Brian formally and with respect for the office, despite their disagreements with his policies. "I am curious to hear how I manifest within your subconscious. Would you mind sharing your dream with me?"

Brian McDonald had originally had no intention of discussing his dream with Eli and was thoroughly pleased to have found his daughter home alone, but he needed to be sure that Eli would do the right thing when presented with the three gold hairs, so he revised his plan on the spot. "I'd be happy to, young," Brian cut himself off, uncertain what to say next. He was of the generation that didn't understand that they are cisgender.

"Certain expressions come and go, don't they Mr. President," Eli covered, knowing they would continue that conversation another time. "But I'm serious, I really want to know what the President dreamed about me!"

Brian regained his confidence, a repeating phenomenon for all in Eli's presence. They had a certain energy which seemed to amplify that of those around them. The President shifted forward in his chair as Eli sat down directly across from him. "You were in the elevator. The elevator in this hotel." Brian paused and looked even more closely into Eli's eyes. Flora and the guards had disappeared from existence, nothing was more important than his mission to make Eli deliver those three golden hairs to him. "You were holding three golden hairs." Eli, instinctively began to laugh, but successfully mutated it into a cough of surprise.

"How did I get the three golden hairs, exactly?" they coughed convincingly.

Brian was about to burst from the interruption but calmed himself, explaining, "I think it's very important that you understand what to do if this dream comes true, Eli. I need those three gold hairs." Brian's whole plan of manipulation fell apart and he sat in the discomfort of it, too long even for Eli to relieve it.

"Well, sir," they tried, "I will do my best."

The President looked at them and whispered, "I'm not one of those kinds of guys, Eli. Y'know, superstitious. I don't normally worry about my dreams." He looked like a frightened little boy. Eli marveled at their situation. They were sitting across from the president everyone called Boy Face Brian. A social media profile of that name was created to parody the president. It garnered over two-million followers. And here, in this moment, Eli was seeing that famous toddler nose being framed by the most pathetic frown they could remember. "I, honestly, do not know how you got them, but I do know one thing for sure," The President sat up and pulled his face together, "you brought those three gold hairs to me." With that, the President rose, stepped past his daughter and walked to the door. "Redwood."

Officer Redford had moved with the President and was now beside the door. He looked out the keyhole and said, "Um," as he opened it for the President.

"Your food, sir." Morty could barely see over the bags of fish-n-chips piled up in his arms as he balanced a tray of beverages in one hand and a tray of condiments and coleslaw in the other.

"Oh yes!" the President beamed, his hunger overpowering the feeling of naked weakness he had sought to flee.

They all sat down to eat at the large dining table in the living room of the spacious penthouse. All except Officer Amy Nicholson, who stood guard after losing rock-paper-scissors to Redwood. Morty offered to stand guard so the two of them could eat first but they both laughed at him. "Do you even know how to use one of these?" Officer Bill Redford asked as he laid his sidearm on the table. Morty looked down at the gun. "Go ahead, pick it up." Redwood looked around the table, "the safety's on."

"I know it's on," Morty said as he picked it up. "Glock Nineteen Gen Five MOS with a Trijicon SRO. Nice, no need to modify the slide. Standard issue of course, but I noticed you're still hanging on to your Sig Sauer's P Two-twenty-nine DAK, chambered for three-fifty-seven SIG, aren't you Officer Nicholson?" Morty laid the pistol back down in front of Officer Redford, dipped a french-fry in his ketchup and continued without waiting for a response. "I earned my Army Marksmanship Qualification Badge for Pistol at the Combat Pistol Qualification Course with a combined hit count of twenty-eight out of thirty on firing tables one through five. Not that it counts for anything now that I've gone civilian."

Officers Nicholson and Redford both looked at each other, then back to Morty. Each of them had the same thought, that Morty had earned a higher rank than they had. Amy had earned the sharpshooter badge at twenty-five of thirty, one shy of the expert distinction Morty had earned, and Bill "came up short," as Amy often joked at sixteen of thirty, barely qualifying for marksman. No one else understood what was required to achieve such a distinction but all present were equally surprised that Morty knew anything about guns at all.

Flora had begun to realize that there were very few things to talk about with her father now that she had been out of his sphere of influence for the first time in her life. Even the conversation over fish-n-chips confirmed that she and her daddy were no longer the pair they had once been. "Look sweetie," the President foolishly claimed, "I told Morty here to make sure he only got paper straws from now on."

"The decision was made for you by the shop-owner," Flora said, no longer protecting her father's feelings, "as it should be with all corporations and manufacturers of product. It only makes sense to create sustainably if we want creation to continue to exist at all."

The meal continued in silence and Redwood was the first to crack. "This is some good fish-n-chips."

"Yes, thank you, sir," Eli smiled at the President, "and Morty," they added with a nod to the man who had run to get the food. The silence continued. Flora was busy dumping mustard from a compostable container, onto her fries. She picked up three of the fries and held them in front of the President's face. They were covered in bright yellow mustard that dripped down the full length of each french-fry and over her fingers.

"Look, Daddy, three golden hairs, you wan'm?"

Brian McDonald didn't know which feeling was stronger, the anger that arose within him as Flora mocked him to his face or the profound sadness as he realized how far away from one another they had become. He dropped the last bit of fish he held in his hand, a bite just seconds ago he had planned to relish, into the compostable basket that was otherwise empty.

"We're leaving," he announced as he wiped his hands with the remaining napkins, the only unsustainable act he had at his disposal, stood up, and turned to the door, which was checked, then opened, by Officer Nicholson. Officer Redford stepped through first and cleared the hallway, while Morty scrambled to clean up. Flora and Eli motioned for him to leave it, and instead, the three of them quickly gathered up a serving and bagged it for Amy to have in the car, a suggestion she refused as it would interfere with her duty of keeping a watchful eye on the President.

Flora called Amy later that evening to apologize but Amy told her not to worry. She had been able to eat when they boarded Air Force One. The two of them laughed about the three golden hairs, the French-fries and the surprise revelation that Morty was an expert marksman which Amy confessed, turned her on more than just a little.

Chapter 7

President Brian McDonald was now finding himself more upset with his own daughter than he was with Eli, who at least was respectful of him, even when in disagreement over issues that only he, the president, could directly affect, or so he thought. The truth was that Eli had indeed become wonderfully influential in the global sphere. Many of the young people who had been listening to their podcast had shared it with family members and friends who, either by association or direct involvement, had influence on policy in cities, states and countries around the world. Eli had drawn a direct correlation between United States imperialism and climate change in a way that few were able to elucidate. They broke down the carbon footprint left by the machine of the military industrial complex, from the obvious effect of emissions to the less obvious but just as critical damage done simply by maintaining bases throughout the world and feeding the soldiers, officers and other personnel populating those locations. President McDonald didn't trouble himself with Eli, however, and was blissfully ignorant of the profound degree to which they would question his administration's policies in the minds of their followers as well as many of the parents and relatives who had been encouraged to listen to their message.

Flora was having an awfully hard time reconciling her feelings for her "Daddy" and the man who was her president. She still loved her father dearly, despite his political shortcomings, and missed her time with him playing games and watching television reruns, the wholesome, moral content of which, she had begun to wonder how her father had apparently missed. Eli, however, embodied everything she envisioned as pure and honest, values she had thought her father was trying to instill in her. Flora and Brian did not speak to one another for the six months following the French-fry incident.

During that time, a peculiar thing was happening to Eli each time they were alone in the elevator of the Ames Hotel. After pressing the button for the floor they desired, for an instant Eli thought they could see a person dressed in old-fashioned clothing, insert a key into a keyhole they had never noticed before on the elevator panel. After turning the key, the apparition would take hold of the rail that surrounded the elevator and the elevator would jolt, as if the very mechanisms which moved the elevator between the floors had become old and unsteady. The elevator would then travel to the floor Eli had originally pressed. The doors would then open, and if no one else was present, this elevator operator would motion toward the open door with his hand. If others were waiting to gain access to the elevator, the operator would vanish completely.

Eli had told Flora about the occurrence the first time it happened, and she asked them if they could try it together. The elevator functioned as usual and no operator appeared. This happened each time they tried together, but each time Eli tried alone, the operator appeared. Eli had begun attempting to have a conversation with the operator since the second appearance, to no avail.

A great many things had happened on the global scene politically and environmentally in the six months since Flora had seen her father and now Eli's vision in the elevator was freaking her out. She wondered if Eli were dying. She had heard of people seeing the ghosts of loved ones before they died and believed the same may have been happening to Eli, but they were in great shape. In fact, Flora had never seen them cough or be short of breath or infirmed or fatigued in any way, period. Eli was "fit as a fiddle," an expression Flora had picked up from the television reruns. "You're in better shape than anyone I know except for Amy and Julie, and they train daily," Flora puzzled as she attempted to explain the operator phenomenon. "I simply can't imagine what is happening to you, Eli," she frowned, "and I'm scared."

"Don't be," Eli immediately responded. "Things like this happen to me all the time," they smiled, "haven't you noticed?"

Flora had never really put together the various, seemingly unlikely situations that involved Eli, which were typically resolved in their favor. Once she did this, however, Flora realized that Eli had to either be the luckiest person on Earth, a magician, or a real-life superhero. This only made her love them more.

Flora and Eli's relationship was romantic and sexual. They had promised one another that they would do their best to focus on studies and limit the amount of time they spent exploring each other's sexual desires. That policy lasted for the first thirty minutes after the moving crews left the apartment on their first day of living together. If they hadn't both been quite brilliant, they would have lost their scholarships. After realizing the reality of the situation, they settled into what both considered to be a perfectly reasonable schedule of sex and studying.

In addition to their undeniable attraction to one another, Eli and Flora were a magnet to other students. Everyone around them could sense their devotion to humanity and its place on earth. Although they were great enthusiasts for climate responsibility, they were not so far gone that they proposed the idea that humanity was some sort of virus the earth was better without.

In addition to their videos on climate, Eli made videos about racial inequality. Eli had done a considerable amount of work exposing the unrightful deaths of people of color at the hands of law enforcement on their YouTube channel, but it was their actual friendship with people of color that showed the nature of their character.

Ella and Fitzgerald, and yes, they get that all the time, were the "poor, distressed people of color, lowly grant recipients, and token black friends of the nouveau riche," an expression Fitz reiterated often, while physically punctuating with quotation marks. Although originally rooted in sarcasm, the description was pretty much right on, for both. Ella and Fitz weren't a couple when they first arrived at BIT. They had both applied to BIT, were accepted, and were offered roughly half of what it would cost to attend, in scholarships. That wasn't enough for either of them to enroll because they could not afford the other half, even after loans, which were also less available to people of color, despite their greater need. BIT thought it would be good for publicity to have a small dinner where Ella and Fitz would be presented with the award by the students who had created the Boston Institute of Technology Scholarship Swap Program or BITSSP.

Flora and Eli thought it was a horribly demeaning stunt and wanted no part of it. They had fully intended to grant their scholarship money anonymously, but the school leveraged the celebrity of the two freshmen to ignite a sort of philanthropic fireworks display, raising over thirty million dollars for BITSSP. Many years later, it would be revealed, that most of that money went to fund the program's infrastructure. Focus groups, determining the appropriateness of need, community outreach research, eliminating certain less promising demographic areas of the world, and salaries and bonuses for the good men and women who work so diligently, "Finding the finest minds of today, for tomorrow," BITSSP itself absorbed the lion's share of the money raised. These good men and women were predominantly Caucasian and were deeply concerned with the plight of the underprivileged.

Fitz had been the subject of such deep concern all his life and was extremely annoyed by it. He explained his frustration during a meltdown in the Student Union when responding to the question of why he was here, posed by the president of the LGBTQ Union, Nightingale Star, a gender fluid grad student who had created their own major in Organic Technology, five years before Eli chose it as their major.

"I have had it with white people," Fitz extended his hands, palms down as he sought to calm himself by signaling those around him to remain calm. "And no offense to my black brothers and sisters, but my older brother would still be alive if our own culture was more tolerant. Billy, my brother, was gay and they killed him for it. In the end, it was my uncle who caused Billy's death." Fitz wiped his eyes. "All because he couldn't keep his thoughts to himself." Fitz began to feel self-conscious, like he was taking up everyone's time with his story and he wasn't even gay. What he saw, however, was deep empathy, first in Nightingale's eyes, then in the eyes of the others who surrounded him and instead of feeling scrutinized, he felt accepted.

"Uncle Al was one tough dude. Big military career and then championship level MMA fighting and teaching. And fans and followers like you wouldn't believe. And all that time Al was bad-mouthing gays and the whole gay culture. Nothing neutral, all in your face crap. Really uncool.

"Well, that didn't stop my brave brother from coming out. And Al would talk shit about him same as any other gay. Three years into it, Uncle Al's MMA class beat Billy to death. They thought they were doing what Al wanted them to do. They thought his anti-gay diatribes were lessons in purity, and that he saw his nephew as a scourge on his reputation.

"The truth was quite the opposite. Uncle Al had been hiding behind his talk for decades, from the moment he had his first crush, through his military career and even in the ring. He fantasized about being with other men but never acted on his desires. The assholes who killed Billy didn't come forward for two months after they beat Billy to death." Fitz shivered, "Their confession, and their reason for killing Billy, drove Uncle Al to take his own life."

The LGBTQ Union was quiet. Nightingale Star was silent.

"I lost my brother too." Ella broke the silence. "He wasn't Albino, like me. No crazy, white-skinned, devil-daughter of a fictional white father, that which so many of my fellow students have accused me of being. No criminal, no druggie, like my poor cousin Derrick, hooked on drugs simply because he sustained a football injury, lost his life because of a stupid game. No, Nathan was just shy.

"The cruelest thing about this society we live in is ignorance, compounded by fear and what that does to the hearts and minds of the pure." She removed her hat and sunglasses to reveal white hair, fine and curly, and eyes that seemed to reflect every light source. Her beauty made her words even more devastating.

"My little brother took his own life, not because he was gay, but because he had seen what the other kids had done to me. He did not have the courage to look in the eyes of those who might attack him. He did not have my strength." Ella's eyes were now swimming in her own tears, the reflections spilling down her cheeks, "he didn't have my strength, because he never asked me for it. I would have given it to him freely, with my whole soul. I would have given him my life." "So instead," Ella wiped the tears from her cheeks and once again turned full circle, to address everyone, "I give it to you."

She hadn't missed any signals, she hadn't disregarded any pleas, they simply never happened. Her brother had gone through his struggle alone, by choice. His suicide note had pointed out the hypocrisy of his own community of color. Choosing to hang himself was a message to those he grew up with that the views from which they measured the worth of their fellow men was not limited to race but was limited by their own rigid perspective, rules and dogmas that had been created by human beings, enforced against other human beings, for the glory of the unknown. Nathan had written that it was his belief that whatever God they had sought to please could not be a god with whom he wished to spend eternity.

"I will not allow my brother, Nathan, or any of my brothers and sisters, regardless of the choices they have made or the reality they are born into, to be left without a voice of love, telling them they are welcome." Ella wanted to give whatever she could, and her enthusiasm became contagious.

It did not take Fitz long to introduce himself to Ella after the meeting of the LGBTQ Union, even though he felt as though the circumstances of their acquaintance seemed opposed to romantic suggestion. "Fitzgerald Franklin," he bowed as he approached her. Ella had been surrounded by students who swarmed her after the meeting. "Ella Robinson, I presume," he continued as she reacted with a smile, "the other recipient of the privileged white kids guilt fund, otherwise known as BITSSP."

Fitz engaged in sarcasm as often as possible because it was his way of handling that which was true. It was at that moment that Ella introduced Fitz to Eli and Flora. She had met them because she had attended the BITSSP award dinner and Fitz had not. He had never seen either one of them before, other than on the internet, and admitted to them that, out of context, they looked like every other white person. Fortunately, they were able to quickly identify the relentlessness of his sarcastic wit and embraced Fitz as the necessary voice of black truth. "I just gotta say that's it more than ironic that you two extremely white people gave the first BITSSP award, a gift from white people to people of color, specifically because they are people of color, to the whitest black girl I have ever seen."

Chapter 8

It was St. Paddy's Day in Boston and everyone was wearing green, even those without a drop of Irish blood running through their veins. Megan Moran was Irish to the extent that her family hailed from County Mayo and her grandmother had introduced them all to dillisk, whiskey and Catholicism, none of which had been Megan's cup of tea. That, on the other hand, was something she enjoyed in the typical Irish fashion, black tea with whole milk and sugar. She didn't know if the milk was a genuine, original ingredient within the ritual of Irish tea-time or if grandma had just been too poor to use real cream. Megan had wanted to bring Irish soda bread to Boston for the family to share, but America had become a land of over-reaction and fear since the attacks of September 11, 2001 and she wasn't even allowed to bring a muffin she had baked for her breakfast through the gate at the airport the last time she flew to Boston. So instead, she bought fresh ingredients and an iron skillet upon her arrival in the city that brought revolution in the form of a tea party.

Flora had not expected St. Patrick's Day to become a shared holiday of the McDonalds and the Moran-Andersons, but her father surprised her with a sudden request to join Eli's parents in celebrating the day with them. The truth was that Brian McDonald had been living every day since the French-fry incident with the unshakable feeling that his opportunity to capitalize on Eli's good nature and proximity to the elevator was in jeopardy. He also felt that Flora was more likely to be civil with him if Eli's parents were present.

This was true.

Flora and Eli had visited the Moran-Andersons in Minnesota a dozen times since the French-fry incident and she had grown to love Eli's parents as her own, in fact, more than her own. They had shared Thanksgiving and Christmas with the Moran-Andersons, toasted New Year's and even enjoyed a romantic getaway on the North Shore for Valentine's Day, Eli's mother's favorite holiday. Their solar-powered car had proven to be inexhaustible. In fact, Eli had been approached by automotive companies hoping to license their patents on the solar array conversion hardware and software, and ultimately, the new plant-based battery Flora had developed since enrolling at BIT. They decided to license the technology to the whole world for free. This was another reason for the President's visit to Boston.

"So, Mike," the President started the conversation around the dinner table, "any chance I can get you on my side of this IP issue with Eli?" Mike Anderson stared blankly at Brian. It wasn't that Mike didn't understand the President; he just didn't share the philosophy that he had any control over decisions his child made as an adult. "Let me attempt to convince you." Brian emptied the butter dish of the remaining butter, mashing it into his boiled potatoes as if the force applied to the potatoes would help the concept sink into Anderson's brain. "Eli has created a vehicle that will revolutionize the auto industry, if my friends in Washington permit it. And that's a pretty big if!" This was a point that both Eli and Flora had considered, but hearing the President address it specifically, as the very first issue, highlighted its importance as a barrier to their generous solution to the unsustainable use of fossil fuels by the auto industry. Brian knew he wasn't going to convince Mike Anderson to interfere on his behalf. He was establishing the foundation for a conversation he was planning to have later with Eli. "The only way we can make this thing happen for the kids is if we work together. And the only way we work together is if this thing makes money."

"There it is!" Flora cut off her dad. "Morty!" Her eyes rolled slightly back in the direction of Morty, who sat at the smaller table, behind her, with Redwood and Kareem Abdul Jabbar. "How long have we been sitting?"

"Two minutes and thirty-four seconds, Flora." Morton Fedelstein catalogued nearly every movement the President made. He agreed to be chipped with the highest security interface with the Pentagon's database. It not only records everything he sees and stores it; he is incapable of turning it off. The President made an announcement when it happened. He made a point of ensuring the world that their secrets would always be safe in the hands of America and in the interest of transparency and cooperation, Mr. Fedelstein would only be present in meetings with foreign powers and dignitaries who had signed an agreement, that he could be in the room with the recording implant running, beforehand. He then urged other nations around the world to sign on if they wanted to get on his schedule for some very big things that were about to happen. As anticipated, this parsed the various nations around the world into two categories, those who would bend to the President's will and those who would not.

Morty also signed with a major media network. They bought the streamed video from the Pentagon after a delay in which anything determined to be of national security had been removed. People sat and watched what Morty saw for hours on end. Amy and Morty had started dating and were now a celebrity power couple. Amy admitted to Flora that the idea of everyone in the world being able to watch them having sex turned her on immensely. She had admitted that to Flora while Morty was sitting next to her on the couch, so the whole world got to see her admit it. This made her profoundly popular. The President erroneously believed he was always the center of attention and that Morty and Amy were along for the ride. Morty looked at the President a lot, so Brian thought the show was all about him.

"Surprise, surprise, we're all together for less than five minutes and my dad wants to know what's in it for him." Flora had become Brian's biggest hurdle since she got out on her own and was allowed to be herself. He had planned to cut her off until she invented the plant battery, as he called it. "The world needs safe energy solutions more than you need more money," she held her fork up high, stabbed through a thick leaf of boiled cabbage.

One-half-hour later, the world would cheer Flora's response to the President, if he hadn't disabled the feed from Morty, using the fob he was issued by the Pentagon. In other words, Brian McDonald could turn off Morty's eyes and ears to the world, but Morty could not. Brian saw this as perfectly natural, after all, he was the President, not Morty, who also saw it as completely natural that he would give up all liberty to serve his president.

The Moran-Andersons were aware of Morty's commitment and would have agreed to allow themselves to be recorded if it had come to it. However, they did not agree with the very principle that it was okay in the first place. They, like many citizens of the world, voiced their concerns about civil liberties only to see no representation of it from their officials, elected or otherwise.

"I'd give it away, too, Mr. President." Mike Anderson never called the President, Brian. In fact, even if Brian had told him it would be alright, which he didn't, Mike Anderson would not have called him Brian. This was partly out of respect for the office, but it was more a way to distance himself from Brian McDonald, the sort of human being he disdained.

"I don't get that!" Brian bellowed. "And I'll tell you another thing, no one in Washington is going to get it either." This was the most salient point the President could have made. He considered himself astute at reading responses to his own words and decided to let it hang in the air. This also gave the President the opportunity to stuff an enormous forkful of an amalgam of potatoes, corned beef and cabbage, into his hungry mouth.

"We don't need Washington to get or agree to anything, Brian." Eli said as McDonald chewed. "In fact, we don't need to be responsible for the actions of anyone but ourselves. By releasing our knowledge freely and without conditions, we enable all people to design and manufacture vehicles that can operate sustainably. There is still plenty of money to be made. It just won't be us making it." Eli smiled as they pointed a finger back and forth between themselves and Flora.

McDonald nearly choked as he swallowed hard, "What kind of sense does that make? You're just shooting yourselves in the feet, cutting off your ears to spite your faces!" He would have gone on describing other foolish acts, but he was fully invested in continuing the constant stream of mashed bliss that had become his flavor of the moment.

"Flora and I are privileged in a way that many people are not. Thanks to my mom and dad, you and Bethany, we get to live pretty care-free lives." Eli explained, "The decisions made by people of color, immigrants fleeing countries because of sanctions imposed by our country's administrations, including yours, the elderly and disenfranchised of every persuasion, are all decisions that Flora and I do not have to make every single day of our lives - what we can afford to eat, do we have gas money, can we even afford to buy a car that will not harm the environment? These are just a few of the problems that the forgotten and overlooked classes face." Eli smiled. They did not judge the President. Instead, Eli saw the world as a wondrous place, full of choices for some. They had made it their mission, from a very early age, to extend the choices of the privileged class to all of humanity.

The President had stopped chewing. "I like you Eli." Brian stood up, reached across the table for the platter of sliced corned beef, added five slices to his plate and sat down. "I like this corned beef. I like the potatoes, and the cabbage, and this hot mustard." McDonald put a spoonful of mustard on his plate. "So, I'm going to share a little "Presidential Wisdom"," the President put down his otherwise preoccupied fork, freeing his hand to make air quotes but not safeguarding those at the table from the corned shrapnel of his alliteration, "People prefer having things to not having things. Nobody wants to give away anything they have gotten used to having and Americans have gotten used to having a lot. We're the greatest nation on Earth for God's sake. You aren't doing a thing wrong by getting every penny you can out of that invention of yours, both of you."

The President had made a good point about Americans. It simply had nothing to do with their decision to provide their intellectual property for free. This was the point Eli was about to make when Flora did it first. "While I would agree with your assessment that, that is the mindset of many Americans, I would not presume to know how many or certainly not how they can justify that perspective in the first place. Most people I know care about other people and would rather see the whole world lifted up together, even if it's just a little at a time, than for some people to have everything all at once. Even if it was them." Since leaving the White House, Flora had become very good at looking at life from different perspectives, "I'm sure there are a lot of people who don't even realize they have it better than most of the population. Do you even know how many people live in poverty, dad?"

"A little over thirty-eight million, last time I checked," the President had created what looked like a double-stuffed Oreo made of corned beef and mashed-up boiled potato and stuffed it in his mouth.

"Auwwgh, dad!" Flora's eyes had begun to water from the blood in her head reaching the boiling point. She was feeling the loss of her fantasy image of her father. "That's an awful lot of people, dad. How can you not care?"

Brian McDonald smiled as he swallowed the last of the massive, corned cookie. "But I do care." He sat up straight and proudly announced, "That was last year's report, down by a cool million from the year before, even with a population increase, and have you looked at my unemployment rate? You should give your dad a little credit, Flora."

Flora was a quick learner and knew enough to know that her father was taking credit for a global trend that had as much to do with people needing jobs even more than ever, seniors working past retirement, part-time work and full-time work being counted differently from study to study, as it did from his administration's policies, but she didn't feel confident enough to debate him on the topic. "Well, I think you should do more. And more importantly, I have every right to do what I want to do with my invention. And I want to give it away, for free, to anyone who will make it, and make a lot of them." Flora was feeling safe with everyone in the room, so she decided to take one last chance on establishing a connection with the father she grew up loving. "So, daddy, I am asking you to help me make it happen." She had not considered asking her father for anything. She had decided that he was a lost cause a long time before, but something in the moment made her feel otherwise. "I know you're still in there daddy. Somewhere deep inside this presidential façade, Brian McDonald, my daddy's heart is still beating, just like it did when you used to carry me on your chest." Tears began to stream from Flora's eyes, "I want my daddy back." Flora fell apart, like a flower. Her father caught her as she fell weeping into his arms.

All eyes were on the President.

Eli, Mike and Megan Moran-Anderson, Fiddlefart, Kareem Abdul Jabbar and Redwood. The President thought to himself that he was not a bad guy - well, not really. He wasn't a bastard, a jackass, a prick or an asshole, he was just a capitalist, and that didn't make him the devil. "Oh shit, the Devil." Brian said out loud as he remembered why he bothered to come to his daughter's apartment for dinner with her some gender, or not, friend or significant other and his, her or their, he didn't know which, wacko, liberal family.

"What?" They all said to him.

"The Devil, I said." Brian replaced his own verbal history, a practice he had mastered since becoming president, one he had studied for his entire life. "She must think I'm the Devil, I said." The President bowed his head over his sobbing daughter and patted her gently with his fork hand. "There, there my little angel, your daddy is here for you." Brian really did love his daughter. And he remembered the other reason he'd flown to Boston - Eli, the elevator and the three golden hairs. He decided to cut his losses. He raised his head, looked Eli straight in the eyes and announced, "I will help both of you."

Flora heard his words through a muffled haze of despair, as if underwater. She lifted her head from his chest and opened her eyes to see everyone smiling. "You're going to help us?" The President nodded. Flora turned completely, wrapped both her arms around her father and kissed him on the cheek.

The rest of the day turned out to be a wonderful experience for all. The President took everyone out for ice cream. "Last time I was here, I noticed a lot of ice cream places," he said to no one in particular, as he adjusted himself within his seat belt. The limousine felt small with all the extra people in it. "What was that place I liked so much, Feablestone?"

Morty knew immediately that the President was referring to Emack and Bolio's, but also knew that he loved to watch himself on TV, "I can reference the file and play it back for you, sir."

"Make it so, Padawan," the President made the sign of the cross in the air in front of him as if blessing the thought. Everyone in the car broke out laughing for different reasons. The video footage from MEV, Morty's Eye View included the President's visit to a half-dozen ice cream vendors in a single afternoon, and Emack and Bolio's was, in fact, Brian's favorite, "Redwood?"

"On it, sir," the limo McDonald liked to ride around in, while in Boston, was a 2018 Cadillac Escalade stretch limo. Bill Redford loved to drive. Each time he drove the President, was an honor. He had two ways of driving the President. The first, and most common, was to drive the car as if it was a luxury liner in which the President should not even be aware that he is in a car. The second was only performed in emergency situations and included evasive maneuvers, and also, if necessary, Bill Redford was prepared to use the car as a weapon. Redwood had come to understand the various inflections within the President's voice. Depending on how McDonald would say Redwood, Bill Redford knew what he had to do. Today's pronunciation had a nuanced tone, part emergency, part pleasure cruise. Threading the needle with a shoelace in

Downtown Boston on St. Patrick's Day, Bill Redford pulled the Escalade up to Emack and Bolio's within minutes. He stopped the car, opened his door, stepped into the street, adjusted the lapels of his jacket, walked to the back of the car, where he stopped to make eye contact with the driver of the first car lined up behind the limo. Even the jackass three cars back could see that laying on the horn would be not only ineffective but also inadvisable. Redwood continued his stroll around the car, to the staircase outside of Emack and Bolio's, clearing the President's route. Agent Amy Nicholson opened the back door for the President who strode directly to the ice cream.

Mike Anderson marveled at Brian's singularity of purpose. If nothing else could be said about McDonald, his dedication toward his own goals could not be denied. No matter what the situation, the President set his sight on the objective and bulldogged his way toward it, without regard for collateral effects or other people's interests. The stunned state Mike found himself in as he observed the President walking past a line of people, guarded by Redwood in the pursuit of ice cream, was not only clear to Morty but to half the Americans watching at home thirty minutes later. The other half did not understand the bewildered expression on Mike's face as the President urged him to pick a treat. Any thought of joining the back of the line disappeared when several of those who had been waiting cried out for autographs from Brian McDonald. In fact, most of the people in line requested autographs from at least one person in the President's group. If one were to take a head count, Amy would have won but she had to decline because she was on duty. Amy, along with Bill Redford, also did not have the pleasure of enjoying ice cream, because of duty to the President, who felt the American public would get a kick out of seeing him back at Emack and Bolio's.

The debate over the President's line-jumping occupied social media for an entire twenty-four hours, twenty-three and a half hours more than the debate over bombing Syria.

Mike Anderson was bombarded by his fellow activists upon his return to Minnesota. Many suggested that it was his duty as a citizen to point out the line to the President, rather than to simply acquiesce with an order of two scoops of butter pecan in a waffle cone. Others went so far as to say that Mike should have told the President what to do with his energy policy, a conversation he had already suffered through, returning emotionally bloodied to the extent that he shared it with no one. Brian McDonald did not care about the environment. He understood the science and still did not care. Mike Anderson understood the President on a level to which his peers would be unwilling to go; he saw him as a human being. Anderson had returned with a prize of far greater value than any of his fellow activists could have dreamed, but he was not allowed to share it until the President gave the word.

The nice old couple who had been sitting at the table by the window at Emack and Bolio's had planned to abandon their own sundaes, half-way through eating them, but instead, after a moment, cut short by the President's gaze, decided to just take them with them. A small table of teens in hoodies rose in unison to offer their seats to the elderly couple. A flurry of fist-bumps and high-fives ensued between the teens, Flora and Eli. The President was wholly unaware as he tweeted, "Get used to it world. Everyone is going have to get in line behind me - and America. More to come." Brian McDonald then disabled the feed from Morty's brain.

Brian McDonald knew that his agreement to help Flora and Eli was life-changing on a global level. Once again, the President had reacted emotionally, almost involuntarily, and changed his entire position on the issue of climate change. "I'm going to be the best president on climate ever," he said as he proved it by being the best president ever at eating ice cream and still talking, "no one is going to be able to say they saved the Earth except for me."

"That's not exactly why we're doing this, dad," Flora turned from hugging one of the teens as they returned to the street, "it's not for personal gain."

"Look, Flora," Brian balanced a melting lump of Rum Raisin ice cream on his tongue to avoid brain freeze, his lips forming the words around an otherwise immobile mouth, "you may want to give away your intellectual property," he swallowed as he wrestled to retain the ice cream. "That doesn't mean I don't gain a fair amount of leverage with guys like Mike here. This is perfect. Obama got the gay thing; I get the climate. No offense, but I'm gonna go with climate as being a bigger deal."

Flora hated that her father could ruin a good thing. "It's becoming harder and harder to accept that you are my father. The way you look at things is so different from the man I grew up with."

"I'm not the only person who has changed, little girl," Brian let the words out even as he realized the effect they would have and quickly did his best to diminish it, "I mean, Flora, my adult, smart and beautiful daughter."

Mike Anderson felt the awkwardness like wet putty, slippery yet shapeable, "Change is something we all wanted under Obama, but I for one did not see enough." He had done it. He had played the better than Obama card and all eyes were on him. The President had put his phone face-down on the table. Flora had turned her frustrated gaze toward Mike while his wife and Eli looked on. "Just as Flora has changed from your little girl into her own woman, you have the opportunity to change America from a fledgling democracy into a guiding light for the rest of the world and

72

changing her energy policy is the beginning of her growth to adulthood." It was a big concept compressed into a single sentence. Mike knew he could not get the President on board with his own world view, but he thought he may have discovered a way into the person behind the president. "You have the opportunity to guide the nation toward a new responsibility, just like a child takes responsibility for their own life, it is time for our nation to take responsibility for itself. You can be the person who enables America to not only take responsibility, but guide others in the process, just as your brilliant daughter, Flora, has done."

"That was beautiful," Morty said through the stunned silence. "I wish you hadn't turned off my brain, Mr. President."

"Yes, Mark"

"Mike"

"Right, Mike." The President placed his spoon into an empty bowl. "Yes, that, truly was beautiful. And the people need to hear it from me." McDonald saw no reason to remain at the table now that his ice cream was gone. "Write up what he said about America, Morty. And Mike, don't go telling anybody about this until I've made an announcement. There's a few people I gotta get on board before I let the cat out of the bag."

Bill Redford dropped off Flora and Eli at their apartment on the way to Air Force One. The President had insisted that the Moran-Andersons accept a return flight with him. Mike Anderson offered to discuss what a new green plan for America might look like, but Brian napped between Boston and Washington, D.C. and disembarked Air Force One before it continued to Minnesota.

Morty accompanied the Moran-Andersons, his chip engaged, under the President's orders. He assured them that the information recorded would not be for public viewing and had been flagged by the President as top secret. The Moran-Andersons agreed to the request because Brian had assured them that all information acquired would be used solely to provide a critical backstory to his negotiations with the key players in energy, the fossil fuel industry. This made perfect sense to them. The first of the President's questions surprised them, however.

"Is Eli a boy or a girl?" Morty asked, knowing that McDonald would take his job away if he had exercised common sense on the President's behalf and simply skipped over the question. Morty already knew the answer, as did most of America. Morty understood that Brian was among those members of society who find it difficult to process the notion that gender identity is how one feels in relation to being male or female - and there are different terms, descriptions and labels for different types of gender identities. "You don't have to answer any questions you feel are inappropriate." Morty offered.

The Moran-Andersons smiled, looked at one another as if to ascertain who would speak first, then responded in unison. "Agender."

Morty smiled in return. He knew that the answer would infuriate Brian, who would not understand its meaning and that he would end up in the exact same situation he would have been in, namely explaining the meaning to the President. However, in this case, having asked the question, he would not lose his job. Each interaction Morty shared with Megan and Mike made him appreciate them more. He looked at the list of questions the President had texted and continued. "How did they come up with the idea to build a solar powered car?" Morty had substituted the correct pronoun in the place where the President had written he/she.

"They grew up with us," Megan answered candidly. "Don't get me wrong, Eli is a genius, neither one of us could come up with the designs Eli dreams up, seemingly without effort on their part, but the reality that we all share a planet and are responsible for what we do to her, well that's inescapable."

Morty quickly followed up with the next question on the list, realizing it was another generic question that couldn't possibly help the President sell the fossil fuel industry on the adoption of solar powered vehicles, "Do they ever talk about me, I'm sorry," Morty corrected himself, lifting his eyes from the text, "Do they ever talk about the President when he isn't around?"

Again, the look between the parents, "Not really," Mike offered as he rubbed his chin, "but they do, occasionally wish out loud that Brian was more like Flora. You know, more aware, maybe that's not the right word. Caring. Yes, I think that's what they mean, caring. Eli is all about other people, always thinking of ways they can improve the lives of others."

The three of them spent the remainder of the flight going through the President's list of questions. A list that turned out to be of a more personal nature than any of them had expected. They were questions one parent might ask another if their children were dating, which was true of Eli and Flora. It had never occurred to Mike, Megan or Monty that such questions might be of interest to the President. By the end of the flight all three had gained greater insight into the mind of the President and each confessed that they had not anticipated that he would be willing to take on the fossil fuel industry on behalf of the revolutionary technology Eli and Flora were proposing. Morty offered to have a limo drive the Moran-Andersons home from the airport but they preferred using the light rail system, putting their money where their mouths had just been.

Chapter 9

"Biotech Brian, that's what they're calling me," the President gloated, "and I didn't even have to lift a finger." He was sitting in his limo with Mitch Hudson, a trillionaire about whom, scant little had ever been written or reported.

He had never been seen in a grocery store, by anyone, ever. No one who had ever worked for or visited a hardware store, movie theater, pharmacy or hospital could remember seeing him. There were the usual records for Hudson, birth, education, fraternity membership and even tax records, though none of the doctors who were at the hospital at the time of his birth remembered participating in his delivery. His fraternity brothers remember him as gregarious and accomplished though not even one could describe his appearance, other than to say what a great looking guy he was.

Every single image of Mitch Hudson throughout all systems, government, finance, education, shared one characteristic, they were all blurry. This phenomenon happened often and in real time. When he had his photo taken for his driver's license, the woman who took it remarked as to how nice it looked, which she validated, as an expert who had seen thousands of such photos in her experience. She told him twice how nice it looked, and that the light that normally flattened out everyone else she took pictures of, somehow managed to make him look even more handsome. Even before the next applicant stepped up for their photo, she had forgotten what Mitch Hudson looked like. The photo itself, saved to the system as a blur within the outline of a man's head.

Two months after having received that license, Mitch Hudson was pulled over for speeding. Hudson admitted to losing track of how fast he was going, smiled, and handed over his license to the police officer. She informed him that she would be writing him a ticket and would return from her vehicle shortly. When the officer got to her car and pulled up the database, the image of his license on her screen was blurry. She compared it to the license she held in her hand which, at first, appeared blurry. Suddenly, she recognized Hudson on the license and paused. She thought for a moment about how handsome he was, something she, as a lesbian, didn't find herself doing with men very often. She turned to her dashboard monitor and saw the same handsome face, clear as day, which she chalked up to loading time issues on her system. The moment threw her off her game and she lost all passion for writing up a ticket, something she normally enjoyed doing upon pulling over middle aged white men. She returned to Hudson's car to find him relaxed and smiling. She felt oddly soothed by his smile and fully captivated by his eyes. Officer Lewis handed Mitch Hudson his license and returned to her vehicle. She sat in the driver's seat of her car and blissfully watched Hudson drive off.

When his car had sunk below the horizon, Officer Lewis became aware of her surroundings.

She was sitting on the shoulder of the highway, the blurry image of what was presumably a man named Mitch Hudson displayed upon her monitor. She felt hungrier than she could remember feeling in a long time. She turned off her monitor, flicked on her lights, and floored it to the food oasis. The fact that she never passed Hudson before reaching the oasis, an odd fact due to the speed at which she had traveled in her pursuit of cheeseburger, never even crossed her mind.

"I'm telling you Hud, you sure made my life easier with the way you handled your petroleum guys. Brilliant move, space." The President was referring to the favor Mitch Hudson did for him by convincing the top executives of all the major oil companies to go along with a plan to divert petroleum consumption away from the consumer and to the newly formed Space Force. By doing so, Brian was able to make the announcement that he would be fully supporting the transition away from fossil fuels to green energy, a mission fueled by the innovations pioneered by Eli and his daughter Flora. The media and the public ate it up. In the end, it was more sleight of hand by President McDonald, working his magic on the public, and this time, on his own daughter.

"That kid of yours is no slouch, Mac," Hudson poured two whiskeys from the limo bar, handed one to the President and toasted. "Let's hope she doesn't catch on too soon, for your sake."

"Not a problem," Brian said as he slugged his whiskey down in one gulp, his customary method of consumption. "Besides, this shift is going to make some serious differences show up in the data these energy geeks keep shoving in my face. It'll take years for them to figure out what's going on. They'll be too busy patting themselves on the back over the reduced carbon footprint of the auto industry to notice. Meanwhile we'll be halfway to colonizing Mars."

"Mars is a pipe dream, Mac."

"You know that," McDonald poured Hudson another whiskey, "and I know that," he poured himself another, then raised his glass, "but the taxpayer will gladly pay, blinded by their love of science, JFK, and good old American ingenuity!"

The men laughed as they let the warmth of the whiskey sink in.

"Flora's going to know better." Mitch Hudson couldn't keep himself from stating the truth that McDonald felt in what was left of his heart.

The President poured himself another whiskey, knocked it back and grinned through the rush of the alcohol, "I'm just gonna have to burn that bridge when we come to it." He poured two more whiskeys. "Tits?"

"Tits," Hudson cooed.

President McDonald pressed the button that caused the window between himself and Bill Redford to open, "Tits," he said, then he toggled the window closed.

Morty, who was seated in the front seat of the limo, between Redford and Amy Nicholson, smiled broadly. In fact, all three individuals, who were seated up front, smiled happily when they heard the word tits. Redford smiled because he liked tits and knew that he was about to be seeing lots of them. Morty and Amy, on the other hand, were smiling for an entirely different reason. Whenever the President said the word tits, he would disable Morty's link to the Pentagon. While it was true that the link had already been disabled by the President, due to the nature of the meetings he had with Hudson, "Tits" meant that only Redford would accompany the President into the gentleman's club. This practice had been established even before Morty and Amy had become an item. Both Brian and Amy were uncomfortable with Amy's presence within the club, so McDonald relieved her of her duty, entrusting his security solely to Redford when in the establishment. Morty had told the President that he wasn't much of a strip club kind of guy, so he stayed in the limo. It was in these moments that Amy and Morty had gotten to know one another better.

After Morty and Amy started dating, the dynamic became even more interesting for the loving couple. Not only was Morty's link disabled, but the limo was spacious enough to accommodate all seven-foot-two-inches of Amy's fit and fabulous frame, enabling the lovers to satisfy their desires in one of the safest places on earth, fully bulletproof with pitch-black tinted windows. The sound system was state-of-the-art and there was plenty of chocolate, a final pleasure Amy regularly enjoyed after coitus. Redford always beeped a signal to Amy when the President was ready to leave, giving both ample time to finish up whatever they may have been in the middle of, unless there were three quick beeps, indicating that the President was on the move and time was limited.

This was generally not the case when Mitch Hudson was involved as it was a favorite activity of his to hire every available dancer, at once, to surround the President in a sea of tits, so abundant that he could see nothing else. It was during these moments that Hudson would remind Brian that, as president of the United States, he was the most powerful man in the world. Mitch Hudson would then orchestrate his own objectives, propositioning the President when he was most vulnerable. This was a system that Hudson had engineered during the Clinton administration, one that stretched far beyond the confines of Washington, D.C. Mitch Hudson operated above the fray, enlisting surrogates to do most of his dirty work. He lost one of his major operatives when he had to kill off Jeffrey Epstein, before the sordid trail he left behind could be traced to its source.

The President was still barely keeping afloat when Morty and Amy put the soundproofing of the limo to the ultimate test as their voices cried out in simultaneous orgasm. Morty had earned the moniker of Tarzan, due to his orgasmic moan, from those on social media who chose to watch the X-rated portions of the post-Pentagon stream for which he and Amy had become famous. Amy's fame derived from the things she could do. She was described as a very tall, unnaturally flexible, strong and sexy Emma Peel by so many bloggers that people came to believe that she had actually played the fictional spy in a movie. This would not become true until three years after she left the service. At which time, it was treated as old news, with reporters, bloggers and even a few critics going so far as to say that she had been much better in her previous performance. This did not hurt sales and the argument over her ability to act that transpired on social media moved her into the number one search result position for "Emma Peel," leaving Diana Rigg a distant number two. A variety of men over fifty argued that Rigg was superior, feeling nostalgic, while most of those who would have chosen Uma Thurman admitted that, although Uma was very sexy in a lithe, supermodel sort of way, Amy Nicholson displayed a flexibility and athleticism the other two would have required stunt doubles to perform.

By the time the President was able to resurface from the sea of tits, Morty and Amy were casually sharing a cigarette outside the limo. "That's a dirty habit," Brian McDonald scolded, "put it out and get in the car. We've gotta hurry; it's time to get Mr. Hudson to the airport." Mitch Hudson smiled as Amy held the door open for him. "And find those Cubans I've been saving, I want to send my friend Mitch, here, off in style!" Morty extinguished the cigarette, leaned inside the rear of the limo, and removed a small case from a drawer beneath the seat he occupies when the President allows. He was about to hand the case to Brian before climbing into the middle seat up front, but McDonald motioned him to take his seat in the back. "I want you to tell Mitch everything Macron said when he asked me to turn off your feed." Brian McDonald sat in his usual seat, turned to Hudson and said, "you're gonna wanna hear what Crony had to say about our friend Bib. I swear to God those guys are up to something." Amy Nicholson did a quick sweep around the vehicle, knowing full-well no one came near it while the President was inside the club, but protocol... She smiled directly where she knew Morty would be sitting, though the glass made it impossible for her to see him. Inside, Morty handed a cigar to Mitch Hudson and another to the President. He leaned across the back of the limo, extending a lighter toward the President's guest. He had never failed to have a light since becoming the President's assistant. He didn't know what to say as his lighter clicked but produced no flame.

"Tits up!" Hudson joked as he reached into the pocket of his blazer and retrieved a small, gold object, shaped like a pen. He touched a small pad on the side of the pen and a flame shot from its end. "Not to worry, my good man," he continued as he lit the President's cigar first. Although he could never remember what Hudson looked like when not in his presence, Morty thought in this moment that Hudson was exactly like James Bond. He wasn't like any one actor in particular who played Bond, but somehow managed to be the very best of all of them in one man. "Now, please, tell me all about the dear Prime Minister and our little marionette."

Chapter 10

Eli awoke slightly before noon on a Monday, sometime in March. This was the usual amount of specificity any morning had at first for Eli. Daily clarity became a possibility only after coffee grown by the family of a friend they met through social media. However, this morning, the coffee jar was empty. The carefully harvested home-roasted beans were gone. Eli had known this day would come, not only when they used the last bean but when they finished their last roast. Beans were due to arrive the week before but were slowed by trade sanctions against Venezuela. "I'm going down for coffee," Eli announced to the air around them, listening for a response.

"Get me one." Flora had completely blended in with the couch and popped up directly next to Eli. She had never successfully startled Eli and despite this admirable attempt, her results remained the same.

"I'd be happy to." Eli's head turned slowly to smile at Flora's face, which she had stopped from crushing into the side of theirs, by a fraction of an inch.

"You're sweet," Flora cooed as she climbed over the back of the couch and onto Eli, transferring all of her emotions and expectations away from trickery and into kissing, which Eli accepted while continuing to walk toward the door. She climbed off of them as they reached the door, "I'll scramble up a little tofu and make some hash browns. Don't be too long."

"I won't." Eli smiled with their entire being. Every day with Flora was wonderful. She was entirely unexpected in their life yet absolutely essential to it. They had written a song to her about their feelings but hadn't yet worked up the courage to play it for her.

Flora closed the door behind Eli and watched them walk to the elevator, through the "fish's eye", as they liked to call it. Eli pressed the button to call the elevator and Flora headed to the kitchen to scramble the tofu. Both she and Eli had become vegetarians since the previous Saint Patrick's Day and were struggling with the notion of telling their parents since Megan Moran had made a point of telling the President that he simply must bring Bethany along to the next family Saint Paddy's Day feast, presumably in Eli and Flora's apartment. It was now roughly two weeks until Saint Patrick's Day and neither had mentioned it to their parents.

Eli waited for the elevator. They still felt a little dreamy as the "ding" of the elevator's arrival beckoned them back to reality. The doors slid open to reveal the elevator operator Eli had become accustomed to seeing when they were alone. This time, he appeared freshly uniformed and brighter in general. Maybe brighter wasn't the right word for it, Eli thought, maybe more solid. That was it. The elevator operator was solid. "You're here, aren't you?" Eli asked the elevator operator.

"Well of course I'm here, are you?" The elevator operator inspected Eli.

"I mean, you're solid. Usually, you're not. I mean, like, I never actually touched you, but I just kinda knew you weren't really there?" Eli tried to explain to the ghost that it was a ghost.

"It's quite the other way around, lad. It's you who are finally solid, here," the elevator operator grinned, "now where you wanna go?"

"I was headed down for coffee." Eli reached into their pocket to take a video, thinking that a ghost won't show up in a video and they could prove to the ghost that it was a ghost.

"Of course you were." The elevator operator turned a key and pressed a button without taking his eyes off Eli. "You know, of course, that coffee every day just becomes coffee every day after thousands upon thousands of days, just like pushing these buttons."

Eli realized, at this moment, that they didn't have their phone and that this elevator operator, the one they had seen since moving in, was always in the elevator, that its very existence was being that elevator operator, greeting other ghostly passengers and pressing buttons for them. Eli assumed they were passing through, though some did seem to be neighbors. "I can't imagine."

"No, you can't imagine because you will never have to imagine because of what you are, but I have you as long as you are stuck in my domain, and you will understand my pain."

Ding!

The elevator operator's eyes darted to the door, stunned at the arrival on an unexpected floor. This was "the T" level, Boston's subway system, directly from the hotel elevator. The elevator operator's calls had previously been direct and unalterable. He had not pressed the button for the T. The elevator stopped and the bewildered operator opened the doors. Eli's surprise was as great, but not the same, as that of the operator. The hotel did not have a floor for its own T station because it simply didn't exist, at least not in Eli's experience.

"Coffee," a well-dressed couple stepped onto the elevator. They had the attitude that they needed to be served and that the fate of the world depended on them having their libation. The elevator operator pulled himself together and smiled at the couple, as he closed the doors behind them.

"Absolutely," the elevator operator winced as he pressed a new button on the wall and turned the key. He was not only surprised that the elevator was pulled in an unexpected direction but that he was required to deliver the couple to the world he aspired to live in. "Die in" may be a more accurate way to describe it, but the elevator operator had already died, and that boat had sailed long ago. He wasn't sure how he had ended up in his role as elevator operator, and whenever he encountered someone going to this other world, he did his best to figure out why they were lucky enough to go there, when he was not. "What brings you to the Ames?"

"We're desperate," the well-appointed woman seemed as though she could never have had a moment of need in her life, but something suddenly stunk of death, and she cried holding tightly to the man who accompanied her. "Someone is trying to kill us." The man, who introduced himself as Bruce, confirmed that they were indeed a target but as Eli was fairly certain they were already dead, the actual threat was difficult to ascertain. "Wait!"

"What is it Kate?" Bruce asked frightfully.

"Who's this?" Kate, the well-dressed dead woman, asked as she pointed at Eli.

Eli extended their hand, "Eli Moran-Anderson."

Kate scrutinized Eli further then shook their hand. "Were you sent to help us?"

"I don't know."

"Why not?"

"I'm just out for coffee."

"COFFEE!" Kate bellowed.

"COFFEE!" Bruce also bellowed.

"All right, all right," the elevator operator exclaimed as the elevator lurched to a stop. He looked as though he had been asked to swallow ghost pepper, lemon, and pig anus as he slid the doors open, "enjoy your coffee."

It wasn't just the coffee that made the elevator operator cringe, even though he did hate both the smell and the taste of coffee. It was the other world itself. He was unable to bear the stench of it and he wasn't sure why. He transported dead people to hell hundreds if not thousands of times a day, but this place was different. It was what most Catholics would call purgatory, a sort of proving ground where those whose souls had not chosen a path would go until the final determination had been made.

"Welcome to Starbucks, may I take your order?" Eli barely understood above the sighs of relief from Kate and Bruce who suddenly appeared and smelled remarkably better. They had ordered their coffee without even thinking about where they were. Bruce and Kate smelled coffee, saw the Starbucks logo and felt at home. Eli realized there was a young woman looking directly at them from behind the counter. She seemed very pleasant and Eli wondered if the young woman even knew that she was dead.

"Who? Me?" Eli asked as very pleasant Joyce nodded from behind the counter. Eli thought about explaining the situation to Joyce's stranded soul, but still hadn't figured out the whole thing for themselves and chose instead to order something that resembled their normal coffee and a cappuccino for Flora. They didn't bother to tell Joyce that her place of employment was never before to be found on the other side of their elevator door. They looked back at the elevator and saw the operator staring back at them as he closed the door. Eli half expected the entire elevator to vanish when the doors fully closed but it appeared to remain intact.

"Your coffees, sir." Joyce beamed from behind the counter.

"That was, I mean," Eli gasped, "wow, I might say unrealistically fast, I didn't even hear the milk being steamed"

"That's Stanley, he's our steamer," Joyce explained, "we call him Silent Bob."

Joyce placed a holder with two cups with lids and sleeves in Eli's hands. They took the cups and tried to pay, but Joyce just turned away.

Ding!

Eli looked at the elevator. The operator stared back from within. Eli looked around the coffee shop. No one was paying any attention to them except for the elevator operator. Eli did what anyone else would do and got back into the elevator.

"After thousands of days, coffee is just coffee." The elevator operator closed the door and turned his key. The elevator lurched then went downward.

"Up."

"What?"

"Up. I wanted up."

"Nope"

"What?"

"Not goin' up, only down."

"I don't need anything else; I want to go home."

"No, you don't."

"Yes, I do."

"Really?"

"Yes."

"So what? It doesn't matter what you want. You think I want to be in here for eternity? If I knew how to get off this infernal elevator, I'd have done it long ago."

Ding!

"Here we are!" The elevator operator slid open the doors.

Eli couldn't make out a thing. No phone flashlight.

"Well, go on then," the elevator operator nudged Eli, "I'll hold on to your coffees," he added, a look of bitter disgust upon his face.

Eli stepped forward, into the darkness as the elevator doors closed behind them. Their eyes adjusted quickly once there was no source of light from the elevator. Eli found themselves in what felt like an old, stone mausoleum. In front of them stood a large wooden door. Eli turned to get back into the elevator which had become, instead, a wall of stone. Faced with no other alternative, Eli attempted to open the large wooden doors.

To their great relief, the doors were not difficult to push open. However, night had fallen, and Eli was standing in a field just outside of what appeared to be a farmhouse, unlike any they had seen in Massachusetts. If Eli were to guess, they were standing in the English countryside, sometime in the fifteenth century. The farmyard tools were far from modern, but many appeared to be new. Larping their way through this seemed to be Eli's only option.

If there was one thing Eli had learned from live action role playing, it was to familiarize themselves with their surroundings.

Eli went back through the wooden doors, eyes more well-adjusted to the dark, they searched the room for a trigger or lever that might reveal the elevator. Eli's own footprints in the earthen floor marked a path from the wall, stepping toward their own feet as they tracked their own movements. This was clearly not a secret doorway situation. This was the stuff of magic, witchcraft, or the gods. As they dropped their head in despair, Eli realized they were wearing their Bernie t-shirt. Eli was one of millions who could not understand how the American people could have such a defender of human rights dedicate his life to their needs, only to ignore him and cop to the party line. But Eli sensed that, wherever they were, the division between the classes not only existed, but may be even worse. Despite the oppression shared by the two timelines, nothing Eli was wearing could be found anywhere in the time in which they now found themselves.

Fortunately, upon further exploration of the room, Eli discovered that on the opposite side of the wall they had just stepped from there was an oven. It was surrounded by oven gear and a variety of garments hung about various hooks. Eli quickly changed out of their clothes and fully suited up for an adventure in jolly old England, except for the shoes. Nike, though the name upon their shoes may have been in use during the Renaissance, the material would not exist for centuries. No boots were thrown about, but Eli lucked upon a pair of sandals which, although loose, stayed on their feet. They hid their own clothes in a corner of the building they figured got little use and walked out into the night air.

The sandals flopped on their feet, but they walked toward the farmhouse as quietly as they could. It wasn't quiet enough for the farmer who was still out working at the edge of the woods, surrounding the field. "You there," he said, as what felt to Eli like an unreasonably sharp farm tool was pressed against his back and held there, "Whatchu doin' in my field?"

Eli froze in place, then slowly extended their arms to show they held no weapon. This seemed to satisfy the voice behind them as they felt the pressure ease upon their back.

"Arright now, you turn around slowly and don't do nottin' to make me raise hue and cry."

Eli did as they were told.

"I am of a mind to..." the farmer fell silent upon seeing Eli's face and dropped his tool to the ground. "I'm sorry lad. I mean yeh no harm."

Eli didn't know why he reacted the way he did, but the farmer clearly had the ability to end their life had he chosen to. He stood over six feet tall and carried an immense bundle of broken branches over his left shoulder, his right hand still limp at his side after dropping his weapon, a finely sharpened billhook.

"You've got no reason to fear me, lad," the farmer smiled as Eli dropped their hands to their sides and relaxed. "I'd never have your good parents think ill of me. Now come inside and we'll see to your comfort. Then, you can tell us how it might have come about that you are wearing my clothes."

Beyond the fact that Eli found themselves in another time, they were clearly being mistaken for someone's son and, for the moment, it seemed to be a mistake made to their advantage. The only worry Eli had in dealing with the farmer and his family was their own voice. Whoever it was that Eli resembled would most likely have an English accent, but they could not be certain what kind. Eli's best hope was to keep quiet. Eli hung their head, trying to

91

appear lost and hopeless, realizing that, for the time-being, at least one of those things were true. The farmer picked up his billhook and flipped it up over his right shoulder. He walked toward the farmhouse and looked back to see that Eli was following. When he reached the front of the farmhouse, he swung the bundle off his shoulder and used it to open the door.

"Look who I found," the farmer bellowed to every room in the house. A young woman, carrying a baby emerged from a dimly lit hallway beyond a small hearth where the farmer dropped the bundle of branches. She curtsied, as was customary when greeting those of higher social, political and economic stature. The poor young woman nearly dropped the baby, she was so surprised to have nobility within her own home. In truth, the home was not hers to own. It belonged to the young man she believed to be standing in front of her.

"Young Master," Meredith McConnell spoke with kindness and fear, "what brings ye' here, so far from your manor at this time of night?" Eli now knew their character. Their next move was to uncover the cards they had been dealt. Kindness is rare, and true kindness is rarer still. Meredith McConnell was truly kind, and Eli felt that from the moment she spoke to them. "Are you hungry?"

Eli nodded, a silent, hungry master. They acted tired and a little bit frightened but were neither.

"I've got a little left on the table. I'll just be a minute. Must put the wee one down." She disappeared around the corner from which she had emerged.

Eli looked around the room. It appeared to be as nice as one could have it being an indentured servant. Meredith had done a spectacular job with little means. Meanwhile, her husband was only two feet away from Eli. He was dirty, sweaty, and looked nothing like a person who might be feigning hunger to negotiate their way through an uncomfortable situation. "Well?" the farmer's eyes were set on Eli's body. They looked up at the farmer, wondering what manner of well was being leveled at them. Was this the type of well that meant, I know you aren't the master? Could it be that the farmer was actually the mastermind of this entire world? "Why are you wearing my clothes?"

Eli was relieved though presented with a difficult situation in which nearly every possible scenario ended with their being forced to speak. Every possible scenario save one - mime.

To describe the scene as absurd is not enough to convey the impact upon Meredith when she heard her husband shouting, "Stag!" and saw Eli waving their hands, outstretched, over their head, fingers curled inward, then waving their hands and shaking their head. "No, not a stag." Eli tried a similar pose, going for bear, completely unaware that the species had become extinct due to hunting. "Angry Jack!" the farmer said triumphantly as he leaped into the air, convinced he had solved the issue of what had happened to Eli's original clothing. Kevin McConnell fell silent and extended a gentle hand toward Eli who recognized the concern in the farmer's eyes. "Angry Jack is no one to be trifled with laddie." Farmer McConnell didn't stand on ceremony when it came to titles and honorifics. "You may be havin' trouble with your pa but it ain't worth the dyin' over."

"C'mon now, Master Ian," Meredith motioned toward the darkened place beyond the glow of the hearth. "We're happy to share what we have, and you're welcome to tell us what has happened." Kevin's eyes widened, "Or not, whatever suits ya'," Meredith quickly revised her offer, the mere mention of Angry Jack suggesting misfortune for any who may encounter him.

The three of them ate together. Eli ate slowly and little. Kevin was ravenous but thoughtfully offered everything to Eli and his wife before taking more for himself. He was a large, muscular man who worked hard yet exhibited a gentleness that made Eli extremely comfortable.

"This is really good bread," Eli accidentally said, as much to themselves as to Kevin and Meredith. They swallowed hard when they realized that words went along with what they had been thinking.

"He speaks!" Kevin celebrated as he gripped Eli's shoulder firmly, then gently retracted his hand. He smiled as he turned to Meredith, "and, he speaks the truth! Your bread is as delicious as ever! Can you believe what she does with the pittance she receives from the Lord?"

Kevin dropped his hands to his side and slumped a bit as he realized what he had said, his eyes looking first to his wife. Their faces reflected one another, mouths turned down, eyebrows knit in worried expectation as both of them turned to Eli. It felt like minutes passed as Eli weighed the alternatives when choosing the right expression for the moment. The closer it got to passing completely, the more uncertain Eli became about their choices. This turned out for the best, as their expression became the exact same expression as the one shared by their hosts. The three realized this in unison and burst out laughing.

The meal and the conversation that ensued were far more nourishing than Eli could have hoped. While social media may not have existed in Meredith's time, she did not let that keep her from having her finger on the pulse of village society. Those who worked in the manor were eager to share gossip with those who rarely engaged with royalty. Eli, as Ian, had no reason to take anything

94

personally and soaked in every tidbit of information that would help them in their quest. They fell asleep on the floor, next to the hearth, bundled in a warm quilt, wearing a fresh set of clothes left behind by Meredith's younger brother. At first, Eli was afraid he had died, but Meredith had recognized the hesitation in Eli's eyes and quickly explained that her brother, Brian, was serving Ian's father in the capacity of stable-boy, or had they forgotten?

The following morning, Eli was awakened by Kevin who apologized for being late out to the field but assured the lad that he would work well into the night to ensure a proper harvest. Before Eli could respond, Kevin was out the door. Eli arose from the floor, stunned by the light of the room through windows that were black as pitch the night before. Meredith appeared, bathed in the light bursting through from the tiny kitchen, her satisfied baby, snuggled in her arms. Eli was amazed at how quiet the infant was, their only experience with other babies having been significantly more audible. "How are you feeling Master Ian?"

"Much better, thank you," Eli responded truthfully, their whole being adjusting to the environment of Medieval England, while wondering how likely it might be that they would run into the actual Master Ian, who happened to be a runaway at the time. It was entirely conceivable that the real Master Ian could walk through the very door they were leaving by. "I must keep moving," also true, "and please tell Kevin that I am so grateful." Eli waved a lot from a short distance away from the front door. Meredith waved once then continued to hold her baby with both hands as Eli continued to wave. Eli didn't want Meredith to know that they were going to double check for the elevator before committing to finding an alternative way back to the future. Eli became uncomfortable waving and dropped their hand into a shrug. "I think I might have left something in your shed. Do you mind if I look?"

95

"It isn't my shed Master Ian," Meredith laughed at phony Ian like he was the silliest person she had ever met. "It's yours, do what you like." She turned away, laughing to herself and smiling at her baby, preparing for the wonder of sharing every new day and each new discovery with him.

Eli was now feeling guilty that they didn't tell Kevin and Meredith the truth about who they were, but they hadn't said a single word that wasn't true. They also knew that the deeper truth was that neither Kevin nor Meredith would be able to understand what had happened to bring Eli to their home in the first place because Eli themselves didn't have the answer. The best possible thing that could happen now would be for the elevator to be back in the shed.

It wasn't.

Eli stood in the shed, staring at the wall for some time before committing to embracing the situation they were in. It hadn't been a dream. They were clearly larping, without the "r", or the "p," although a fair bit of both would certainly be required. Eli put themselves into the shoes of young Ian in both plan and action. Postulating that he would be something of a pampered young man, Eli considered that Ian may return home sooner than later and that two Ians would be harder to explain than an Ian with memory loss. Eli would become Ian to anyone who would ask, but they would act as though they had been through a terrible ordeal and lost their memory. They may not be so successful in posing as an Ian who is healthy of mind. So, a fair bit of amnesia when confronted would certainly be the best play. Traveling away from the master house would lessen the chances that they might cross paths with the true Ian.

"You are not from around here," Eli heard Kevin's voice say from behind them and slowly turned around. He was holding Eli's Nike shoes in one hand and his billhook in the other. "And you are not Ian." Kevin was sweating from work. He did not appear aggressive, intimidating or anything but stunned. He was like a young child seeing the beauty of a rainbow for the first time. He held the shoes forward, "How?"

It didn't take long for Eli to recognize and understand the awe Kevin was experiencing, but they didn't want to jump to any conclusions. "What do you mean?"

Kevin was clearly holding in a world of questions as he extracted the one that made the most sense to him to ask first. "How are these?" He dropped the billhook and rubbed his fingers across the surface of the shoes. "What are they made of?" He turned the shoes around, as a pair, examining them in the light of the morning sun through the open shed doors. "How can anything be so bright and full of color?"

"India." Eli answered without hesitation.

They thought it was a good answer until Kevin said, "What is India?" Eli hadn't noticed before, but Kevin had a sack across his shoulder which he now, slowly lowered as he gently placed the shoes in front of himself in order to reach into the sack. "Is this from India?" he asked with the same wonder.

"You know my father," Eli realized that Kevin wouldn't know about India because Britain had no interest there yet, and even as tuned in as Meredith was, she had no clue about foreign policy anyway. "He has some powerful friends. People who do a lot of traveling." Kevin looked up at Eli and down to the sack, the shirt, then to the shoes and finally back to Eli. "I felt out of place wearing them," Eli answered truthfully.

Kevin pulled the shorts, socks, everything out of the sack and put them on the shoes. "I want to see it." Kevin looked more fragile than he did the night before. Eli could feel concern in Kevin's eyes. There was something weighing upon Kevin.

"Okay, I will do it. I will dress in these clothes if only you tell me what troubles you, first." Eli was feeling good about remaining Ian with Kevin and was confident they could pull off the whole India thing, but something was nagging at Eli since they stepped off the elevator. They didn't know why they were here, or even where here was. Eli didn't fool themselves about what they were doing. They had gotten on the elevator when they saw the operator and weird things had been happening, so they could have avoided it, but something was driving them to get to the bottom of the mystery behind the elevator operator. "I can see that you are frightened by something and I don't think it's the clothing my father gave me, or India, or anything to do with me really. So, what is it?"

"The crops are goin' ta fail." Kevin hung his head. He was still on his knees beside the sack. He crumpled to the floor like a tired little child who couldn't walk another step. "The spring is all dried up."

Ding!

The elevator doorway appeared on the wall of the shed.

"C'mon, I haven't got all day." The elevator operator called from within.

"A deal's a deal," Eli held a finger in the air toward the open elevator door and stripped down to their boxers and binder as the elevator operator looked on without expression. Kevin didn't know where to look and was confused by everything he saw. "Everything is going to work out, Kevin." Eli stepped into the shoes to complete their ensemble as Kevin's eyes rose to see Eli, dressed as they had arrived. "No time to explain," Eli couldn't help but laugh to themselves just a little. "I have a strong feeling we'll be seeing one another again soon." Eli left the clothes they had borrowed in a heap where the shoes had been and ran for the elevator as the operator closed the doors.

"I wouldn't bet on anything if I were you," the elevator operator moaned. "Going down."

Chapter 11

Eli felt terrible that they left Kevin staring at a bare wall in the absence of an elevator he never knew had been there, despite working in proximity to it since he had been a child. They had left Kevin with a glimpse of the future that he would now have to decide to share with his wife Meredith or keep to himself.

It was at the moment of drawing his breath to holler her name that Kevin saw a small and very orange disc on the earthen floor of the shed. He bent close to observe it before picking it up, uncertain that doing so might not trigger the appearance of another door. Kevin picked up the disc and examined it even more closely. It had a small letter "m" printed on it. He thought about the fact that he was holding an object in his hand, the nature of which he hadn't yet determined and that it was monogrammed. He had only seen monogrammed anything in the hands of or worn by royalty. Kevin knew there was a difference between his life and his means and that of the master, but he was fairly certain that neither of them could disappear into walls.

Kevin placed the small disc into a pocket in his shirt, resolved to the notion of telling Meredith the entire story of what had happened with the mysterious visitor, after he had the whole day to make his own sense of it.

"Where and when was that floor, exactly?" Eli asked calmly as they held their hand out to receive the coffee cup being offered by the elevator operator.

"I just push the buttons, lad."

Eli felt the elevator shift this time. Without confirmation or acknowledgement of any kind from the elevator operator, they muttered to themselves, "We're going sideways."

Although the description of the motion was not entirely accurate, it was perhaps the best way to describe the result.

Ding!

The door opened.

Eli saw before them a wall with a massive gate. They had noticed that the coffee still felt warm in their hand. "It's still warm." They looked to the elevator operator for an explanation.

"Of course it is." The elevator operator looked annoyed and motioned toward the gate with his other hand still holding the other coffee with disgust.

"I'm not going anywhere." Eli sipped their coffee and continued, "the last time I stepped out of this elevator I found myself in another time. I'm staying right here and drinking this coffee."

"Stay here, go there, it's all the same to me," the elevator operator said as he pressed a button with his other hand and Eli found themselves standing in the road which led to the massive gate. They felt as though they were still in the time of Kevin and Meredith but in an entirely different place. The elevator and its operator were nowhere to be seen and Eli was standing in the middle of a dirt road wearing clothing, and holding something in their hand, for which the essential elements had not yet been invented.

They decided to walk to the gate rather than run to the woods and hide. Better to face the reality of the situation despite its apparent lack of foundation. Eli had learned to embrace many things in life over which they had no control. Their attitude was that life needed challenges to remain interesting. Still uncertain whether or not this was all a dream, Eli decided to approach the situation as they had so many before, with optimism and cooperation. Although their efforts didn't always bear fruit, most outcomes had been positive.

Based on the success of becoming Ian, Eli decided to go with traveling eccentric nobility with amnesia for five hundred. They laughed to themselves as they remembered watching reruns of the game show Jeopardy with their parents, Flora, and the President. Their parents had learned to let the President answer out loud and first. Brian McDonald could have easily won the game show, rarely missing an answer, but for those he did miss, others in the room had remained silent.

Eli looked over the entire gateway before approaching. They kept a close eye on the top of the wall, larping all the way. The Nikes on their feet were shining very bright. Eli stepped up to the gate and called up to the sky, "Hello there, hello there!"

"State your purpose here." The call came back from high above through a window by the gate. "Now!"

Eli had an uncanny knack for sensing things within a person's voice, and although urgent, the voice above them did not seem threatening - if anything, it felt disheartened. "I am a traveler," Eli said and added, "I am not here to sell you anything, and I seek only knowledge."

"Stay where you are," the voice called back, no more threatening than it had ever been.

Eli stood and waited for what felt like an exceedingly long time. They finished their coffee and thought about the fact that there wouldn't be a recycling bin and that the material for that had not yet been invented either. Eli had spent a great deal of time informing the world about the plastic industry through their blog but had somehow managed to allow their own uses of it, except of course, for straws. Eli was so wrapped up in self-evaluation over personal use of plastics that they hadn't noticed the displacement of a sizable chunk of stone brickwork or a man standing in the hole left by its displacement.

"What manner of creature are yeh ven?" The man stepped out of the shadows but kept a hand on the open door made of stone.

"Human, my good sir," Eli answered with a British accent they picked up from watching reruns of the Avengers, the latest White House favorite, plus it had worked with Meredith and Kevin.

"Ven what is it vat you might be wearin', if you don't mind my askin'?" The man was motioning toward himself. "Someone will fink you daft, boy," the man continued as he held a finger to his lips, confirming what Eli's father Mike had told them, that putting a finger to one's lips dated as far back as ancient Rome.

"They're from Rome," Eli said hopefully as the man lead him inside with an amused shrug. "Are you interested in fashion?"

"Oh no, not me, maybe vuh missus, but I ain't got vee eye for it." The man was shorter than Eli by a whole head and smelled a bit like alcohol. "No, I just got no one to talk to is all." The man motioned toward a small grouping of stools and a table, tucked into a nook in the stone hallway at the base of the wall. Eli could see the long staircase to the outlook platform where the man had been stationed at the window. "Nobody comes to town no more, not since vee apples stopped growin'." Eli sat across from the man who bowed slightly, "name's Faddeus, Faddeus Muversbeard."

"Eli Moran-Anderson," Eli extended their hand. The man looked puzzled. Eli didn't know if it was an issue of timing or class assumptions, but it was clear that shaking hands with Eli was a matter of some consideration for Thaddeus. "I am pleased to meet you," Eli left their hand extended.

"I am sorry, sir. I d-d-did not," Thaddeus stuttered, "I am not, I mean, of course, sir," he shook Eli's hand, "It is my honor." Whatever Thaddeus Mothersbeard thought Eli to be, he would be treating them with respect. Eli sat at the small table and placed his cup from Starbucks in front of them. Thaddeus looked more closely at the cup, then at the Bernie shirt. He leaned over until his head was horizontal so he could look again at Eli's shoes, noticeably wincing at the flesh of Eli's legs, puzzling over the shorts, and inspecting the printing on the Bernie shirt, with respect and curious astonishment.

"Are you guarding the town by yourself?" Eli realized the question seemed more loaded than they had wished.

"No, vere are guards all along vuh wall but vey're probably all nappin'" Thaddeus grabbed his own mouth to silence himself and laughed. "Tea?" He placed a small cup in front of Eli, then poured from a small pot. "It ain't hot but it tastes good and it's easy t'brew." Thaddeus pointed further down the hallway. Eli turned to see sunlight streaming in through a small portion of the outer wall that was missing its stones, illuminating a row of glass jars in which tea was brewing. "I like to add a little somefin' extra vat vuh missus cooks up." Thaddeus pulled a small flask from his waist and poured some mostly clear liquid into his own cup. Eli held up a palm.

"No thank you, Thaddeus, I believe the tea is the right tonic for me." Eli was certain that Thaddeus was the key to their return to the elevator, but they didn't want to spend another night away from Flora. "It's very peaceful here."

"Peacevul, ha!" Thaddeus laughed as he drank. "Dead's more like it."

"So, you're dead?" Eli said impulsively, after all, it wouldn't be entirely out of the question given recent experience.

"Bah-ha-ha-ha, oh, you're a funny one boy," Thaddeus had decided that direct from the flask was the tonic for him. "Sir, I meant sir, your majesty. Wait," Thaddeus looked more closely at Eli across the small table, "what exactly are you?"

Eli had been asked this very same question more times than they cared to recall, but they imagined this inquiry to be prompted by a different sort of concern, "As I have told you, I am a traveler," Eli remained cautious despite the man's drunken condition.

"Well, vat still don't quite answer my question now do it?" Thaddeus was becoming zeroed in on Eli, the haziness, clearing from his eyes as if looking into Eli's very soul. He had taken a small knife from a belt around his waist as he leaned even closer to Eli. Thaddeus brought the knife up to the table in front of himself, the blade side held between his thumb and forefingers. He used the handle to punctuate his words as he spoke. "I am finkin' vat you are no evuhday travluh. I know vis because I have seen travluhs evuh day!" Thaddeus laughed heartily at his own joke until he abruptly stopped. "But the travluhs don't come no more, and now 'ere you are, shiny as a bug, callin' up to me and wakin' me from my nap!" Eli wanted to tell Thaddeus the truth. He seemed drunk enough to forget but clear enough to strike.

"We do things a little differently where I come from." Eli decided to make Thaddeus work for it.

"Y'said vuh cloves are from Rome. Well sir, I have let travluhs from Rome ride in fru vuh gates more van once and notta single one of

105

vem was wearin' anyfin' like what you are wearin', right 'ere in front of me." Thaddeus stopped waving his knife handle in Eli's face to reach into his pocket. Eli leaned back cautiously but did not run. Thaddeus stared intently into Eli's eyes. "In fact, the only fing I have ever seen vat is as shiny as you is vis!" He pulled from his pocket an unimaginably shiny, golden apple. At least Eli had never imagined such. Eli gasped. "Right, m'boy!" Thaddeus grinned, "Vat's what I'm talkin' about! Tell me it ain't so." Eli stared at the apple. "Y, can't take yer eyes from it, ken yeh?"

"No." Eli was mesmerized.

"Do yeh want to hold it?" Thaddeus offered the apple. Eli accepted. The apple was heavy. It was solid gold. The apple Eli held in their hand was worth a fortune. "Nobody knows I have vis apple." Thaddeus smiled as Eli handed it back respectfully. Thaddeus had trusted them with a possession that could change his life.

"Why don't you sell this apple?" Eli inquired as the apple left their hand.

"The apple don't belong to me." Thaddeus responded without hesitation. "It belongs to vuh town and I protect the town." Eli was impressed if not confused by the loyalty of Thaddeus.

"Then why do you not tell anyone?"

"Because it is the last." Thaddeus put the apple back in his pocket, "and I mean to protect it until vat glorious tree starts growin' vem beauties afresh!" Thaddeus held the knife directly in Eli's face, the handle resting on the tip of his nose. "And vat brings me to you." Thaddeus spun on his stool and tossed the knife into a darkened alcove of the hallway. Eli heard it strike something behind them as they watched a smile form on the face of Thaddeus. They turned on their stool and after their eyes had adjusted to the light, saw where the knife had struck. Against a wall of stone leaned an old wooden door, one hinge rusted off, the other gone entirely. In front of the door leaned a broken wagon wheel, a perfect target, like a dartboard for knives. The wheel was splintered along every facet, the wall behind riddled with chips, gouges and scratches of every kind, but Eli could not find the knife. They looked back to Thaddeus who was still beaming. He simply nodded back in the direction of the wheel. Eli turned back to face the wheel but still could not see the knife, so they stood up and walked in the direction of the wheel until their eyes were at the proper angle to see that the knife had passed through the hole for the axle and was firmly lodged in the door behind.

"Awesome!" Eli shouted, overwhelmed with the accuracy. They turned with arms raised in celebration, cheering for Thaddeus, "Well done!"

Ding!

Eli turned as the elevator door open behind them. They turned once again back to Thaddeus, whose eyes widened, then settled into a smile. "Time to go." Eli heard the voice of the elevator operator behind them as the smile on the face of Thaddeus grew.

"I knew you weren't from around 'ere!" Thaddeus pulled the apple from his pocket, "Some fings are hard to explain. Looks like you must be goin'"

"Looks like!" Eli waved as they turned toward the elevator, "and thanks for the tea!"

"Safe travels, Eli." Thaddeus tossed the golden apple from hand to hand as he watched the doors of the elevator close.

Chapter 12

The elevator operator handed Eli the other coffee from Starbucks. Eli noticed that it was still quite warm to the touch. "How?" They said, as much to themselves as to the elevator operator.

"Not exactly your everyday elevator," the elevator operator winked. It was the first direct, eye to eye contact the two had ever shared, "but I imagine y'know that by now. And I must tell you, now that we have reached the end of the line that you are a far sight calmer than most who end up here. I wish I could tell you more, but considering things can get much worse for me," the elevator operator looked down and pressed the button to open the door. "That's hell for ya, right?"

Eli had questions they wanted to ask the elevator operator now that he decided to say more than a few words, but there wasn't time. There was a sound from outside the elevator door. It wasn't the usual Ding! It was more of a gong, a large and well struck gong, and the door opened.

Eli stood in awe of a vast chamber with a wide staircase leading down from a balcony just outside the elevator, the appearance of which had changed to luxurious and ornate, with a hint of gaudy. They suddenly felt odd carrying coffee in a disposable cup.

"Aren't you lovely, you brought me coffee!" A voice rose from below the horizon of steps as Eli ventured toward it. The voice sounded older, wiser, and very soothing. "I think it would be an absolutely perfect time to meet, neighbor." The woman behind the voice moved angelically up the staircase and suddenly Eli felt heat like they had never encountered in their life. Searing, bone evaporating heat, so intense and so quick that Eli had nowhere to run, hide or shield themselves from it. Just as suddenly, the heat moved inside of Eli, who could no longer feel the surface of their skin, but before their brain could think they must be dead, and quite probably wrong in their skepticism about the existence of hell, the feeling vanished. Eli felt no heat. Eli felt no pain. Eli touched their own skin and felt nothing. "It takes a little getting used to," the old yet radiant woman smiled warmly as the gong finally fell silent, "so does the gong!" The woman took the to-go coffee cup from Eli and drank. "Ah, I love a good dark roast," she smiled as she looked thoughtfully at Eli.

"Pardon me," Eli said, unsure of their own voice, "but I don't think I'm meant to be here."

The old woman pointed to the spot where the elevator had been, "Oh, you're definitely meant to be here. That damn thing doesn't show up unless someone's meant to be on it." She surveyed Eli more closely, "But, I have to agree, you're in the wrong place. In other words, you're meant to be here, but you don't belong here." The woman laughed to herself, "I am inclined to think he doesn't even know you're here." The woman had moved halfway down the staircase while speaking and Eli had moved effortlessly with her. Eli was conscious of walking but felt more as though they were gliding.

"Who is he?" Eli asked half suspecting they had been mistaken about the existence of the Devil. They thought of saying they had been dead wrong all along. Eli laughed at their own thought pun then immediately deconstructed the nature of a pun as a play on words that are normally spoken or written and began an internal argument over whether thinking a pun was even a thing.

"My grandson." The old woman answered, which still left Eli wondering, both about the pun and about the existence of the

Devil. "He's probably out causing trouble, as usual, but you'll meet him soon enough."

It hadn't occurred to Eli that they might actually be dead and in hell until the old woman said the part about meeting the grandson, they had assumed to be the Devil. The thread of a possibility that there could be such a being would normally have sent a shiver up Eli's spine, but they felt nothing. This made them even more suspect of their own reason.

"Why don't you sit down and tell me about yourself, Eli." The woman motioned toward a chair in a spacious living room with the oddest sense of décor they had ever seen. "Unless of course, you've changed your name again," the Devil's grandmother smiled as she sat across from the chair. Eli sat. Very few people outside of the Moran-Anderson family knew that Eli was born Eleanor and that Eli had asked their parents to officially change it on their behalf at the age of five. It had never been the subject of any of Eli's videos, but they intended to make a video about the subject after being encouraged to do so by Ella and Fitz. Eli sat silent across from the woman who also sat silent.

"Oh! Right! Sorry," Eli said, remembering they had been asked to tell their story, presumably regarding how they had come to be sitting in the living room of the Devil, in conversation with his grandmother, by his grandmother, and that their silence had become awkward. "Well, I got on the elevator to get some coffee, because mine ran out, and Flora asked for some, so I went out to get some and now you are drinking her coffee, which stayed remarkably hot given the fact that I spent at least two whole days away from her and home, and now I might be dead."

"You aren't dead, sweetie," the Devil's grandmother replied. "I've seen 'em dead before, and you aren't. I can't quite remember how it is you are able to sit here with me; it'll come to me. But go on. And this time, don't try to do it all in one sentence. Breathe, I'm not going anywhere." The Devil's grandmother made Eli feel very comfortable given the situation.

"I'm not sure what to say," Eli confessed, "I mean, what exactly do you want to know about me? I told you how I got here, and you already know my name."

"Liberace!"

"No."

"Not you, Eli, I know your name isn't Liberace, but that's why you're here." The Devil's grandmother did her best to describe what had just sorted itself out in her addled mind. "You're one of my special babies, just like he was. I protected you."

"Protected me? From whom?" Eli felt that the woman was sincerely confused, "and I know who my parents are, so I'm sorry, but I'm, well, not your baby."

"Of course, you aren't my baby, Eli, it's a figure of speech, you see. You are my baby because I protected you from everything, not just from my grandson." The devil's grandmother was quite clear now, her own plan being realized before her eyes, she continued. "Just like it was for Liberace, dear boy, when he came to play for my Lucifer."

Eli gulped like a character in a Chuck Jones cartoon as if swallowing the truth of their own situation might help them to accept it. They were indeed speaking with the Devil's grandmother, sitting in the Devil's home, presumably hell, listening to a story of Liberace performing for Lucifer, the Devil himself, from the lips of a kind, beautiful, old woman who claimed to be their protector. "So, just to recap," Eli ventured a summary, "You are the grandmother of the

111

Devil, who some call Lucifer, others Satan or Beelzebub, and you live with him here, in hell. And Liberace, a legendary piano player who lived in a time when admitting to being gay was akin to admitting to some sort of crime, came here to play for the Devil. And in some way, I am related to Liberace because you protected both of us from the Devil. And yet, here I sit."

"Correct," the Devil's grandmother calmly replied.

"Okay." Eli stood up and began to pace. "Is that why I'm here, so you can tell me some fantastic story about Liberace playing for the Devil?"

"No, Eli, even though it was a beautiful and spectacular performance, and I would be happy to tell you all about it, if you'd like, no. I am not the cause of your presence here, you are. There is something you are meant to do."

"It couldn't be." Eli buried their face in their hands, "The dream."

"What dream?"

"The President's dream, Flora's father, Brian. Brian McDonald, he's the President of the United States, anyways, he had a dream, something about three golden hairs."

"That'd be it, then," the devil's grandmother jumped in. "This President of yours is in trouble. Believe me, I know who Brian McDonald is and exactly why he sent you here."

"But I'm not here for him."

"Yes, you are," the Devil's grandmother had her moments where age and the mind play tricks and blend details into a waterslide of doubt and uncertainty but in this moment, she was clear. "He wanted you to come back with these," the old woman threw her head to one side and gathered her hair to reveal three fine, shimmering, golden hairs growing from just behind her ear and she plucked them from her own head. She held them forward. "Take them."

Eli looked at them in dismay, "But, I'm not sure I want them. I don't know that I want to help that man with anything."

"You're a fine human being, Eli. You don't even see the power in having these hairs and that is why I give them freely to you. And don't worry, they'll grow back. What you do with them is entirely up to you, but at least if you take 'em you got 'em."

Eli took the hairs from the devil's grandmother. "Thank you."

"Don't mention it." The woman smiled and held up the to-go cup she had been sipping from for the length of the conversation, "after all, y'brought me Starbucks!"

Eli wound the hairs around their fingers and placed them into their sock as the two laughed at the terms of the exchange.

"Now," the grandmother asked in earnest, "what else can I do for you?"

"I don't think I need anything, except to get home," Eli quickly responded.

"Are you sure? I have a feeling there's more, and I'm usually right about these kinds of things." The Devil's grandmother took another sip from the to-go cup.

"Well, maybe I don't need anything, but I met some people on my way here."

"And?"

"And I'm not sure what kind of help you are offering but they need some big help, like, life-changing, force-of-nature stuff."

"Devil's Gramma," the Devil's grandmother used both thumbs to point to herself, "right there with ya!"

"Well, okay then. Meredith and Kevin need water for their land. I don't even know when they, if they are alive," Eli stumbled through their request because they had no understanding of what was happening to begin with.

"Details. No problem, what else? Grams is here for you, sweetie."

"Thaddeus has the last golden apple from a tree his village depends on for their livelihood. He protects it until the tree produces again, rather than take it and cash it in for himself. Something is stopping the tree from bearing the golden fruit and the town is suffering. But I can't tell you where the village is located because I got there by elevator."

Gong!

"I hate to do this, Eli, but I've got to turn you into an ant," the devil's grandmother placed her hand on Eli's shoulder before they could respond. Eli became an ant, just as the old woman had said. She held Eli in her fingertips and placed them upon the seam of her dress, just behind her neck from where she had pulled the golden hairs just as the Devil appeared at the top of the staircase.

"I'm home, I smell human..." Lucifer barely touched the stairs as he descended the staircase, "and Starbucks?"

"New arrivals," the grandmother responded as she reached toward the floor. She grabbed a latch and pulled up a trap door from which a pillar of flames erupted then subsided. "No one special, just the usual. The guy was a CEO from an insurance company, and the woman was either a TV star or a movie star, I can't remember which. She was convinced that her agent would be able to clear everything up and the guy did the usual song and dance about what good business means and how everyone confuses being a good businessman with being a good person and that sometimes the two simply cannot coexist." She made a face like she had swallowed a bug, "he had pumpkin spice in his coffee."

"Reason enough!" Lucifer laughed heartily as his grandmother handed him the to-go cup she had taken from Eli. "Still hot?" he asked.

"No, and I drank most of it, but it's dark roast, and no pumpkin spice." She took the cup back from Lucifer and suggested, "why don't you sit down, and I'll brew you up a fresh cup of unsustainably-sourced, unfairly traded, Satan's roast from Ethiopia and you can tell me all about your day." She closed the trap door as the two of them made their way down another staircase to a room where a large, ornate, yet exceedingly comfortable chair awaited the Devil. The grandmother turned toward a bar on one side of the room, the others walled completely by windows that looked out on a chasm with walls of human flesh, writhing in a sea of flames. "Cappuccino or espresso?"

"Espresso," the Devil responded cheerfully, "and make it a double!" He pressed a button on his chair and speakers within the ceiling burst forth the sounds of agony rising from the undulating landscape of fallen souls. "It wasn't a particularly fruitful day, but I did have quite a laugh in Golgotha."

"You keep going back there. Your fascination with the whole Jesus thing is getting repetitive. I feel as though you're limiting yourself. You need to get out and try new things."

"You're right, Grams. That's why I visited a new place today, somewhere different, sometime different." The Devil bounced a little in his chair, "I went to the future."

"You didn't!"

"I did!"

"But Lucifer," the grandmother said apprehensively, "don't you remember what happened the last time?"

"Aww, Grams, this is different, I promise!"

Like any good grandmother, the Devil's grandmother only wanted the best for him, the things that would bring him the most joy, and sometimes those things were quite terrible. Eli listened as she scolded Lucifer for preventing a war that would have killed hundreds of thousands, bringing hatred, disease and famine in its wake. "Imagine the greed and deception that would have unfolded. All of that anguish wasted because you thought he would notice and allow you back. He's never going to let you back my little Lucy."

"I know that now, Grams, and I hate it when you call me that!"

"Well, I won't call you that when you start listening and stay out of the future! Now here, enjoy your espresso." She handed the Devil a fresh, hot cup of espresso and said softly in his ear, "and remember, darling, you 've still got the past."

"And the present!"

"It's all the same to you my little one." The grandmother beamed as she stroked the hair of the Devil. "You're always so clever, like that time you stopped the apple tree from growing golden apples."

"I had nearly forgotten that one." The Devil pressed his nose between his forefingers and thumb and shrugged his shoulders and the tree appeared through the windows, like they were some immense crystal ball, "look how it droops, leaves barely hanging on and no apples, no blossoms, a village in misery simply because I invited a wee family of rodents to live in the roots of that once magical tree. One of his, no doubt. Where he plants joy, I bring suffering. Absolutely brilliant if I do say so myself!"

"Which was more brilliant, my dear, sweet, Lucifer, depriving a village of gold or robbing them of their water supply completely? I seem to remember you leaping about the place over a river you managed to clog in a truly unexpected fashion," the grandmother encouraged the Devil to revel in his deceit and trickery.

Lucifer grinned, placed a hand to his forehead, then looked through the windows upon a vast river valley with no river. The river itself seemed to have no origin for as far as the eye could see, yet the valley it had carved was clear. "To think this devastation all grows from a single source," the Devil gloated, "who would believe there could be such idiocy among humans? I mean seriously, this is one humdinger." The Devil loved having his grandmother around to talk to about himself. Half the time, she was delusional and beyond that, she was forgetful, so most of the time he told her stories, they were brand new to her. "They would all have water if it were not for a single toad. You see, the water once issued forth from under the ground, sufficient was its flow that it did fill all the rivers and streams in that vast valley. One day, I was watching a toad repeatedly attempt to enter the hole, only to be pushed far away by the flow. Three times I watched as that toad hopped back to the source of the waterflow only to be forced away each time. I wondered to myself why a creature might want to force itself into such a tight space when all around it already held such beauty and life. So, I decided to give the toad its wish. The next time that little bugger tried to get in that hole, I suppressed the flow just long enough for that pudgy little toad to force its way to the other side of that hole. Then I released the water and what do you think happened?"

"It got stuck."

"Exactly, that pudgy little toad tried and tried to get back out of that hole 'til he died, sealing up that water supply for good. Well, good in my book at least. The people in that valley suffered terribly. One by one, families had to leave their homes, children crying, old people dying, all because of a pudgy little toad. And what do they all do? Those humans? Do they look for the source of the problem? No, they chalk it up to God's will. There they go again, givin' credit where it isn't due. I'm the one who put the damn toad there, not him, not the All Mighty!" The Devil held his hands tightly against his forehead and the view changed. It replayed the toad inching its way toward the hole then going through and getting stuck. The Devil turned to his grandmother, "did you see it, did you see how the water stopped Grams? That was me. I did that, not Mr. Willy." The Devil laughed an almost pitiable laugh as his grandmother soothed him with gentle fingers and supportive words.

"Of course it was you, dear Lucifer. But how is it that the water did not flow again once that toad had died and decayed?"

"Oh, my precious grandmother, I am so glad you asked." The Devil joyfully recounted his handiwork while it came to life behind the walls of glass at the pull of his chin. "There, you see, Grams? I sent a herd of wild horses through, just north of the ridge causing an avalanche and sealing the spring once and for all. Do you know how many of those pathetic humans offered their souls to me if I would just help them to survive, from those who worked the land to those who were in command, every last one of them at my mercy. In a deal with the Devil, the Devil always wins, and I can tell you I made some sweet deals when that river valley ran dry."

"You are indeed powerful and clever, my dear grandchild, and I wish I could give you all the admiration you deserve, but I have something better. Today is a fabulous day, not only in total deaths but in percentage acquired." The devil's grandmother put a hand on each shoulder, put her face close to her grandson's and hollered, "sixty-seven percent!"

The Devil hit his feet so fast he nearly knocked his grandmother through the glass walls that were his crystal ball. But he caught her, apologizing profusely as she steadied her stance. "Mea culpa, mea culpa! Show me, Grams!"

The Devil's grandmother clicked a button on a remote she drew from within the folds of her housedress and the coffee bar rotated out of the room to be replaced by an illuminated board that blinked the number sixty-seven followed by a giant percentage sign. "Today is a great day for the Lord of the Underworld," the grandmother said in her best game show host voice. "It's not quite the haul you made on September Eleventh, Earth year two-thousand-and-one, but you know what you always say!"

"Anything over Fifty!" The Devil smiled, wrung his hands with glee and embraced his grandmother. "The numbers have always been in our favor, Grams. Jesus knows, and I have tried to convince the big idiot."

Satan wept.

"Oh, knock it off, you big faker!" The Devil's grandmother slapped him across the face so hard it nearly spun his whole head around in the other direction. They both burst out laughing.

"Well, time's a wastin'." Again, the two erupted with laughter. Eli wasn't sure why the Devil thought that line was so funny, but the grandmother's confirmation made them think that they were laughing at the notion of time, in general.

The Devil walked through the glass surrounding the room, the crystal ball's view changing to the mass of writhing humanity in turmoil. He turned back toward his grandmother with the look of a child stepping into a candy store. The Devil drank in the despair, like the scent of sugar in the air. He appeared to melt into the molten flesh like lava consuming and incorporating everything that surrounds it, never again to cool.

"Now!" the Devil's grandmother shouted as she transformed Eli to their original species. "You must leave, before he returns," she urged as she pressed a button on a wall that had not been there a moment earlier.

Gong!

The elevator materialized directly in front of Eli. "Going up!" the elevator operator called out until he saw the Devil's grandmother standing by the button. "A pleasure to serve you, Madame," he said respectfully as he smiled. Eli detected a longing within him, beyond the yearning to be free of his perpetual servitude as the elevator operator.

"Take good care of this one," the grandmother instructed as Eli stepped onto the elevator. The doors remained open for longer than usual. "Well, go on then. He'll be back soon, and it wouldn't go well for this one to be around when he does!"

The elevator operator pressed the button to close the doors, his head following the opening, his eyes never leaving the Devil's grandmother, until he could see her no longer. "You must be special indeed. Lots come down, but I count only two since I've been here who have gone back up." The elevator operator turned to face Eli, "Her Highness spoke to me, I am at your command!"

Eli thought about the notion of time and then, didn't. If they were correct, it wouldn't matter if they dropped back in on Meredith and Kevin first, because the elevator, like the universe, was timeless.

"The young couple with the baby, I reckon," the elevator operator smiled up at Eli before they could speak. Eli nodded. The elevator operator pressed the button.

"Thank you, Emerson." Eli said impulsively. The elevator operator stumbled like a frightened rat, into the corner of the elevator car, then relaxed as a profound feeling of comfort passed over both Emerson and Eli. "I know your name, though I do not remember you telling me it." Eli tried to explain their feeling of knowing but felt as though something more had occurred.

Ding!

Emerson's demeanor had changed dramatically. He was excited to operate the doors for Eli this time and he smiled as he revealed that they were back in the shed where Eli had revealed the truth to Kevin. It was dark, but this time, Eli had a sense of where they were. They stepped out of the elevator. "Should I stay?" Emerson asked politely.

"No," Eli grinned as they motioned to their own clothing, "I'm already conspicuous enough, and I'm pretty sure I know how this works now." They made a gesture linking themselves with the elevator and then directly between themselves and Emerson as they bowed and backed away.

Emerson closed the doors, and the elevator was gone.

Eli was excited to help Meredith, Kevin, and the mistakenly named Ian, with the pressing problem of no water for their crops. They had decided to return to the day after the day they had left Kevin in the shed.

Kevin had decided to do a little work in the fields, on the crops he kept alive by gathering water from a lake a whole day's ride away. He was in the fields when Eli arrived in the shed. Kevin's spare overgarments were on the same hook as the day before, and the day before that. Eli did the exact same thing they had done two days before, and dressed in Kevin's clothes, they approached Meredith's doorstep. She opened the door to greet them, the baby in her arms and a smile on her face. "You'll have to stop dressing in my husband's clothes, Master Ian."

"My apologies Meredith," Eli answered as they entered the home of the young couple, "is Kevin around?"

"Around what exactly?" Meredith asked as she tried to reconcile the thought of Kevin wrapped around something, anything other than her and her baby.

"Oh, I am sorry, Meredith, it's an expression I picked up from my travels." Eli couldn't be sure about how much Kevin had told Meredith, but he was getting the feeling that he hadn't told her anything that had happened in the shed.

"Well, you couldn't have gotten too far since yesterday," Meredith beamed as she held the baby in her arms, "are you hungry?"

"You'd be surprised," Eli responded, and to their surprise found that they were, indeed, quite hungry. The smell of freshly baked bread permeated the home. "And, I am, yes, I mean hungry, that is." Eli was having a hard time not telling Meredith everything. "I got far enough to discover what is drying up the river!"

It was best that Meredith had just placed young Ian in his crib by the kitchen, because she leapt into the air at the news, but upon landing allowed reason to cause apprehension. After all, Master Ian was there the day before and returned, knowing the cause of their plight within a day. Teams of men had searched for the cause for months. Many attributed it to a light melt, when in truth, the water from the melt was never enough to create the river. But none of them knew this. Most had given up and chalked it up to God's will.

"How?"

"A toad!"

"What?"

"A toad. Well, technically, a dead toad and some horses, wild horses." Eli stated.

"Okay." Meredith responded as she presented a loaf of bread to Eli. They both sat at the small table, young Ian's eyes following Eli the entire time. "I can see how a toad might stop up some water, sure. But all of that water? Folks say it was the light melt." Meredith cut off a slice of bread and served it to Eli on a small plate with a large scoop of fresh butter on the side, it was roughly half the loaf. She stuck the knife in the butter, "I don't see how wild horses have anything to do with it. But that wasn't what I meant when I asked how."

Eli saw the determination in Meredith's eyes. They knew that the truth was absurd, but it felt like the only alternative. "It was the Devil."

Meredith stared at Eli, then looked over at her baby. Young baby Ian turned his head to look at his mother, then returned his gaze to Eli, as his mother did the same.

"Only the Devil knew of the source of that river. It originates below the ground from a single source, through a hole in a vast wall of rock. A toad, repeatedly visited the hole, thinking he might find something on the other side, and the Devil simply let him have his way. He held the water back just long enough for the toad to slip through, and then the toad was trapped."

Eli was about to tell Meredith about the horses when Kevin came in the front door with Eli's shoes. He looked relieved and horrified at the same time because that is exactly what he felt. He rushed to Eli, placed a hand on their shoulder and begged, "Tell her where you are from!" Kevin needed the explanation as much as his wife did, but he felt terrible that he hadn't told Meredith about the nature of Eli's disappearance. He felt so terrible about it in fact that he blurted out, "He's from Heaven!"

While this fit perfectly well with the story, it was not the truth. However, for the time being, Eli felt that it was a better way than the truth as far as it had to do with them. "Hello Kevin, it's nice to see you. Such timing! I was just explaining to Meredith that the Devil clogged up a very important hole and that is why you don't have any water."

"Heaven?" Meredith asked quietly while looking more closely at Eli.

"He isn't from here!" Kevin added.

"I'm not exactly a he either, I'm more of a they." Eli stood up, feeling hulked over by Kevin and scrutinized by Meredith. They began to pace in what little space there was for it in the small home of the overwhelmed couple. Young baby Ian had fallen asleep. "But the important part is that I can lead you to the hole!" Eli was certain that they could describe the area of the origin, provided the vista presented in the Devil's lair was accurate. "We can get the water back!" The prospect that they could have water once again momentarily swept away the absurdity of Eli's presence and both Meredith and Kevin hugged Eli gratefully. Before either of them could formulate a thought about how one might address a being from Heaven, Eli continued, "Do you have horses, people and shovels?"

"I can get them." Kevin stepped back from his hug, "How many do we need?"

"Well, you know what they say, many hands make light the work!" Eli couldn't be certain if anyone had ever said that before this moment in time, but they no longer cared. Eli was going to play angel and do everything within their power to behave like one. "Get everyone you can. Meredith, may I borrow your brother's clothes again?"

"I haven't had time to wash them yet Master Ian." It was at that moment that Meredith realized that the baby she had chosen to name Ian, was named after someone who was not only not Master Ian but was instead an angel whose name she did not know. "What is your name, your angelness," she offered reluctantly.

"I am Eli, Meredith. And I can wear the clothing without a washing, thank you."

"What's this?" Kevin asked as he held up a small object with an "m" on it. He had carefully wrapped it in a small leather pouch he wore on his waist, after deciding to wait to share the news about Eli with Meredith.

"It's candy," Eli responded as they took another "m&m" from deep inside a pocket of their shorts, hidden by Kevin's overclothes and popped it into their mouth. Kevin considered the one in his own hand. "I wouldn't," Eli offered as they handed a fresh one from inside their pocket, "germs, you know." They realized their mistake, since it was most likely that no one of that time even understood what germs were, and continued, "Kevin, have you ever seen an immense rock that looks like an egg with a large crack in it?"

"Sad Chicken Crossing," both Meredith and Kevin responded in an instant.

"That's where we're going." Eli turned toward the baby, "I think Ian's a good name for him."

The most difficult part of the whole situation wasn't explaining who they were or even finding the source of the waterflow problem and resolving it. In fact, everything went very well, and the men of the surrounding area were able to dig down to the source, clear the area surrounding the place where the once curious toad had sealed their fate and restore the underground spring, to feed the river and once again water their crops. The most difficult thing for Eli was saying goodbye to Meredith, Kevin, and Ian.

This time, all three of them watched as Eli called for the elevator, simply by willing it to appear. Emerson held the door for as long as Eli wanted, "Well, I guess it's time for me to go." Eli knew that there was no real time to consider but they couldn't help worrying about Flora being lonely or worse, panicked over their disappearance. "I have another friend I must see before I go home, so, take care of little Ian."

"Thank you, Eli!" Kevin and Meredith responded in unison. As if as an afterthought, Meredith added, "and thank God?"

"It's a long story, but I'll see what I can do." Eli stepped into the elevator backwards, their eyes never leaving the young family until the doors closed.

"Nice couple," the elevator operator said as he closed the doors. "Where to?"

"Please take me to see Thaddeus, Emerson." Eli was exuberant over the fact that Meredith, Kevin and little Ian now had a water source to irrigate their fields, water their livestock, and live from day to day. "Just about the time we left him should work nicely!"

"My pleasure," Emerson responded as he pushed a button and the elevator lurched sideways. "Just out of curiosity, why aren't you going home. I mean, I never got a second chance, but if I did, I'd be home with Lucille, my sweet Lucille."

"Was Lucille your wife?"

"Better." Emerson looked up at Eli with eyes swelling with regret, "Lucille was my Bloodhound. Oh, how I miss her. I could stand this place, this job for eternity, if only I had my sweet Lucille."

Ding!

Emerson wiped a tear from his eye as he opened the doors for Eli, who stepped slowly out of the elevator, "I won't be long," Eli said with an enthusiasm they were trying desperately to instill in Emerson, "I have a plan."

The elevator doors closed behind Eli as they smiled broadly at Thaddeus, who was still tossing the golden apple back and forth between his hands like everything he had just witnessed was one hundred percent normal and expected. From Thaddeus' perspective, Eli had just stepped into an elevator, a thing that did not exist in his time, the doors closed and the thing that did not exist in his time vanished, then reappeared, and Eli stepped out of it. Most people would have dropped the apple by this point in time, but Thaddeus simply stopped tossing it and placed it back in his pocket. "Do you know what's killin' our tree, boy?"

"Sure do," Eli responded happily as they turned around, stepped toward the wall behind where the disappearing elevator had been, bent low and retrieved the knife from its target, the bullseye within the wagon wheel. "Turns out you have a rocent problem. By the force of his will, the Devil drove a family of rats to the best location to drain your tree of its very life. The longer they make their home there, the sooner your tree will die."

"So, we kill the rats, and we get our gold apples back?" Thaddeus got up from the table. "Hand me m'knife boy, I got rats to kill."

"I'd prefer a more humane solution, more of a drive the rats away type of thing." Eli countered as they brought the knife to Thaddeus.

"Humane?" Thaddeus looked at Eli like they were from another world. Eli made the knife disappear, rather than handing it back to Thaddeus, a trick they had learned by watching a fellow YouTuber. It would have been more surprising, perhaps even impressive, if Eli hadn't just travelled through time in a disappearing elevator, just seconds earlier. "They're rats, boy. Give me my knife."

Eli realized that Thaddeus was dealing with a much bigger issue than a family of rats and their safety. His entire town would disappear if the tree were to die. Eli handed Thaddeus the knife, "Save your town, sir!"

Thaddeus did not wait for Eli to leave or follow. He ran to the tree.

Ding!

Emerson's cheeks were still wet from his thoughts of Lucille when Eli boarded the elevator.

"You said something about a plan?" Emerson looked hopefully at Eli as he closed the doors.

"Certainly," Eli beamed, "but first, I'm going to need some coffee."

Chapter 14

Flora was still browning up the hash browns to a nice crispy edge when Eli stepped through the door to their apartment. The smell was inviting, and Eli was hungry again. They carried the coffee into the kitchen and placed it quietly on the counter. While Flora had no luck in surprising Eli, the same was not true the other way around and scrambled tofu was jettisoned from the frying pan as Eli slipped in behind Flora and hugged her.

"Oh my God!" Flora gasped, then quickly settled into the hug. She turned to kiss Eli and saw a different look in their eyes, deeper, more serious than usual. They kissed her passionately as the tofu and hash browns sizzled in their pans.

Pulling back slowly, as if their lips had become a single unit that they were working to carefully separate into two halves that had not yet been clearly delineated, Flora and Eli looked at one another, then at the pans, then back at one another, "foods!" they said in unison.

Eli told Flora everything that had happened over breakfast and hot coffee from Starbucks.

"So, when are you going to tell me that you realized that this was all a dream?" Flora had been listening intently and recognized the passion in Eli's voice but was having a hard time processing all that Eli had told her, and she knew that Eli didn't believe in the Devil. "I mean, you don't even believe in the Devil, or God for that matter!"

Flora was right and she had every reason to doubt the veracity of Eli's tales, but she couldn't ignore their eyes. She could see the truth in Eli's eyes, and it began to frighten her. "Everything is going to be alright," Eli said as they placed their hand on Flora's. "As I explained, the Devil's grandmother likes me and is protecting me."

Eli retrieved the three golden hairs from their sock and showed them to Flora. She half-cried through her laughter as she realized that her father's dream had been true. She thought of the french-fries and the mustard and laughed even more.

"This is awful," Flora said as she stood up from the table, "my daddy's gonna die and go to hell!" She paced within the tiny kitchen, "No, it's good. He deserves it. He absolutely deserves to rot in hell." She paced more quickly, "He is killing the planet, he hates black people, well, any people of color, and women, not that my mom's any great shakes, but at least she doesn't hate herself. Oh wait, she probably does, I mean I would."

"Flora." Eli responded calmly.

"What?" Flora was shaking, "I am literally shaking uncontrollably here, Eli. Do you realize what this means? Eternity is a thing!" Flora leaned over the table and pointed in Eli's face, "And you met the Devil!"

"I didn't actually meet him. I was an ant."

"Wait! What?"

"The Devil's grandmother turned me into an ant when she hid me, maybe I wasn't clear." Eli rose slowly from their chair and placed a calming hand on each of Flora's shoulders. "I'm not entirely sure he's what we all think he is."

"My father or the Devil?" Flora forced a smile.

"Both, either, I don't know exactly." Eli was still trying to sort out their own feelings from the days they had been gone. It was only minutes for Flora and would have been far less if it hadn't been for the line of the living at Starbucks. "I mean, there was definitely pain, suffering, eternal anguish and despair, but he seemed like a normal guy. I think he might have gotten stuck with the whole Devil thing. His grandmother is an angel. Hell, he was an angel, once upon a time," Eli laughed then realized that Flora wasn't seeing the humor.

"You just told me that the Devil is real, and by the sound of things, my father is going to end up in hell, and you think it's funny?" Flora made her face tight, which when combined with the small nose she got from her father, made her look like a rat. This made Eli laugh again, which only made things worse. "Out, get out of here Eli!" Flora pointed to the front door and stomped her foot.

Ding!

The elevator appeared. It was in the place normally occupied by the refrigerator. The doors opened and Emerson peeked out from behind his corner by the buttons. Flora could see him this time, "If I might have a word?" He motioned for Eli to get in, which Eli did. Emerson closed the doors and the elevator disappeared.

"I thought you might need a little help," Emerson smiled as he pressed a large red button marked STOP.

"How did you know?" Eli looked to where Flora had just been standing, then back to Emerson.

"I don't want you to lose her, Eli." Emerson pointed to his own head, "I thought it might be a bit of a scare to hear the truth about the afterlife and all, and you seem like the type that might spill the beans without really thinking the whole thing through."

"Oh, Emerson, you are the best!" Eli realized the second chance they had been given as Emerson opened the doors of the elevator. He had brought Eli to the moment they arrived back at the apartment. Something was off, when they stepped out of the elevator, they realized that the previous time, roughly an hour earlier, they were holding coffees. Eli turned back to face Emerson, who smiled and held up two hot coffees from Starbucks.

"Everyone deserves a second chance!" Emerson smiled warmly as he slowly closed the doors.

"Speaking of that," Eli became intensely serious, "if anyone ever tries to take the key from you, what do you do?"

"You don't want to see that, lad. It ain't a pretty sight." Emerson's face twitched momentarily into a beastly grin then back to his usual sulk.

"Well, have you ever thought about letting them have it?" Eli asked plainly.

"Oh, I let'em 'ave it alright." Emerson laughed quietly then scolded himself just as quietly, "not okay."

"Emerson, listen to me. All you have to do is let go. If someone takes that key from you, you let them." Eli insisted. "Tell me you will do it."

"Okay lad, I gotta close these doors. Now go back to your lady." Emerson winked and closed the elevator doors.

Maybe surprises are overrated and maybe the truth isn't always the best policy when it isn't asked for. Maybe it would be better to do what they always did when they got to their apartment door and they had things in both hands, and they knew that Flora was inside. These are the thoughts that Eli had as they approached the door to their apartment. So, they knocked on the door with their own head.

"Coming!" Eli heard Flora's voice through the door. They heard the floorboards slightly creak and the lock turn, and in the time it took for the doorknob to turn and the door to open, Eli had decided to keep the Devil to themselves. "You're just in time," Flora pulled Eli into the apartment, "c'mon, I'm starving!"

They had a wonderful breakfast of scrambled tofu and hash browns and decided that they would spend the day together, starting with a walk through the Boston Common. Or the elevator ride down to the street, Emerson laughed with joy, "Kept it to yourself, didn't ya?" Flora didn't hear a word of it or see Emerson at all. She thought Eli was nodding their head out of sheer happiness, something she had seen them do many times.

Chapter 15

Mitch Hudson and Brian McDonald lived in a completely different world than everyone else. Their world was one of their own making. Some argue, the same is true for all people, that individuals create their own realities. The people who argue that are rarely staring into the barrel of a policeman's gun simply because of the color of their skin. And while Brian McDonald wasn't the first President to militarize the police, he was the first to directly profit from it. He wasn't any worse when it came to enabling a racist criminal justice system than his predecessor, he was just a lot more obvious about it, making no apologies when he increased his ownership in the largest private prison firm in the world.

"You know your dad's a total piece of shit, Flora," Fitz said as he rode up on his bike, dismounted it and sat in between her and Eli, seemingly in a single motion.

"What did he do this time?" Flora asked without looking up from her bag of popcorn.

"Hey, Eli," Fitz quickly greeted his friend before continuing, "okay, listen to this, so he is arming the cops and buying up more prisons and calling it criminal justice reform. You know damn well what it is. It's further suppression and incarceration of people of color by the system and by the white man. The big white man with the tiny little nose!"

"I know, I got a call from my mom. She was pissed because he was selling off the shares he bought her in some yoga slash meditation company that apparently made a ton of money off of soccer moms all over the place." Flora looked up from her popcorn, "I really wish I could help, Fitz, but you know he doesn't listen to me."

"Well he did on the climate." Fitz knew he had made a good point, "Maybe you can get him to change his mind about people like me. I mean, we even had a brother in the White House and things only got worse for black people. He isn't helping you out on climate to save the planet and you know it. It's political. If your daddy wants to look even better, he needs to take a stand for equality. If he doesn't do something soon, everything's going to boil over."

"What do you mean by boil over, exactly?" Flora asked what everyone she knew wondered about, what a true revolution might look like.

"People of color not taking shit anymore. But you know it's going to go both ways. If your daddy doesn't shut the white right down, they will make everything worse. There will be violence and fires, shooting and riots, and that's just from the agitators on both sides. What comes after that is going to be worse. The police, armed to the teeth, are going to take over, and then the real trouble begins. But your daddy could stop all that from happening." Fitz truly believed that Flora had the power to influence her father for the better. Even she believed Brian had listened to her and wanted to do the right thing when it came to the climate. She wouldn't learn the truth until later.

"He won't." Eli frowned as they looked at Fitz and then at Flora. "His base is full of extreme white wingers. If he loses them, even Biden could beat him, and Bernie could destroy him."

"Now you know the Dems aren't going to let Bernie get the nomination. Something is going to come along that is going to derail Bernie. Heck, I wouldn't be surprised if Hillary rears her ugly head again." Flora wasn't a big fan of Hillary to begin with but living in the White House intensified the feeling. "Sorry guys, I just, I mean, I am sick over the politics. Why can't they just do what is right and good?"

"Flora, I hate to say it, but you have to admit that your dad, while outwardly nice to Fitz, sees him as less important."

"My dad sees everyone as less important."

"True."

Eli decided to take a different approach, "I am just trying to point out that your father is like many white people who genuinely believe they are not racist. It is not a single act or behavior, it doesn't have to be words, it's an attitude, an ignorance and a disregard that makes them racist. It's an unspoken judgment, a preordained position and perspective that fundamentally creates the unequal ground upon which their racism is built."

"Um, Eli?" Fitz interrupted, "I'm just saying the girl should ask is all."

"That's what I'm going to do." Flora said as she tossed the remainder of her popcorn toward the swans. "We're going to Camp David!"

"Who's going to Camp David?" Fitz asked, half-hopeful, half-terrified. He wanted to go to Camp David just to say that he went there, but he had already been to the White House and the only black people he saw there were in service to the white man. Fitz didn't get to go to the White House until after Obama was President. At the time of his visit he even argued that despite Barack Obama having been the President of the United States, he too, was in service to the white man. Eli agreed and Flora spent most of her time defending Obama. Her arguments were finally put to rest when Fitz began rattling off the number of black men, women, and children who had been killed by cops while Obama was President.

"All of us!" Flora smiled as she wrapped her arms around both Eli and Fitz, "We're going to Maryland!"

"Ella, too?" Fitz inquired.

"Ella, Emmy, Cecilia, Josh, Mattie, Maggie, Priya."

"You're naming everyone in the LGBTQ Union," Fitz interrupted, "What about the Black Student Union?"

"I was getting, there, Fitz, everyone," Ella explained, "We need Jordan, Black Student Union President, Robbie, who organized the coalition to recognize black excellence in science and engineering, Mehta, Chair of Women Seeking Change, every last one of our friends who are working to see the change we want. We are going to bring them all with us. We are going to interrupt my daddy's vacation and make him address this situation now!"

"They're not all going to fit in my car," Eli laughed as they kissed Flora on the cheek, "We're going to need a couple buses."

Flora agreed, "and a permit. I'll call Morty."

"Can you trust that little Saltine?" Fitz had taken to calling Morty the "little Saltine" ever since his visit to the White House when Morty berated half of the White House staff for their inefficiency in dealing with a delegation from Germany. Fitz knew that Morty was a friend of Flora's due to the close relationship she had with Amy Nicholson, but he never trusted him, and not just because he was white. No, Fitz didn't trust Morty because he resembled a character in a cartoon that had frightened him as a child. He could never remember the name of it because he had so completely blocked it from his own mind, nor could he remember if it was a TV show or a movie. Either way, he was pretty sure the guy looked exactly like Morty.

"I don't know why you can't think past your weird association with a cartoon character from your childhood, Fitz. You're a smart guy. All fears and unfounded associations are purely that, unfounded, and a creation of the mind, to wit one must also conclude that fears and unfounded associations can, in fact, be eliminated, purely by force of will, or in this case, a simple act of the mind, namely, forget about it!" Flora had become a fierce supporter of Morty and his relationship with Amy ever since her daddy had implied that he might separate them. Flora had no idea that it was because they always looked happier than he felt when he left the titty bar. "Amy and Morty are friends of mine and will do anything for me because they know I would do anything for them and by extension they will do anything for you." She looked intently into Fitz's eyes, "I know it doesn't always work that way in the world, my daddy is proof of that, but when it comes to my friends, them I can count on!"

"Oh, you know it," Fitz replied as he hugged Flora, "I getcha and I am most definitely down with the whole Camp David thing. Anything I can do, I will do, my friend." Fitz was the most fierce and friendly person Flora had ever met. He was supercharged about whatever happened, be it celebration or protest.

"You have to get everyone to show up while I arrange for the buses and the permits." Flora gave Fitz a kiss on the cheek and they hugged again.

"Where are you going?" Eli asked as they held their phone up to record Flora and Fitz.

"We're going to Camp David." They replied in unison.

"Perfect." Eli said as they pocketed the phone. "I'll post everything the moment we see your dad at Camp David. All eyes will be on us and he'll have no way of backing out."

"Racial injustice has gone on for far too long." Fitz put a fist in the air. He looked at Eli and Flora. They too had fists in the air. "Damn, I wish you two were black right now!"

Chapter 16

"You can't pin this one on me any more than you could the assassination of Martin Luther King or Abraham Lincoln," The Devil was holding up a newspaper with the headline, Washington D.C. On Fire! It erupted into flames as he became more insistent, "all I ever did was give them religion, the rest of it came from humanity itself and even giving that collection of biology a name implies a unity that seems unattainable given their history."

"I never said it was your fault," the devil's grandmother smiled warmly, "I simply mentioned that your latest human toy is the one responsible for turning the situation around, that's all. You're the one who keeps taking responsibility for them. Take Jesus for example."

"Oh no, Grams," Lucifer held a finger up to silence her, "you know He manipulated me. Even Jesus knew it in the end. He wanted that whole thing to happen. I might have given humans religion, but He gave them Jesus. And then that dysfunctional hermit abandoned his own son, just so he could start an empire of fear."

"Don't get started on that again sweetie, I'm sorry," the old woman said, "you can always shift the paradigm if you want. I mean, we've talked about it before, many times. Every single day, in fact, for longer than either one of us can calculate, but you know as well as I do that nothing warms you like the despair of millions of souls. The moment you step into that writhing mass of greed, avarice and jealousy, you come alive. Change is hard, and my dear boy, you are terrified of it. Imagine what is must be like for those weak little white men you continue to put into power."

"They aren't all white."

"They may as well be."

"And I don't put all of them into power. I mean, some of them just get there on their own." The Devil said slowly as if trying to parse the Presidents, Kings, Queens, Tsars, Emperors, dictators of all sorts into those he had put into power and those who had gotten there on their own.

"You are going to hurt your own brain, boy." The devil's grandmother placed a soothing hand on his forehead as he calmed a bit and settled back into his throne. "I know you want to stir things up, go all Mitch Hudson on this one, get your little toy Brian to call out the troops and blast those black people back into place, but part of you wants to sit one out and you know it." The grandmother continued to pat the Devil's head, "Why don't you do it this time? See what President Brian McDonald does all on his own. When he calls Mitch on the phone, don't answer. When he feels the power and strokes that gold pen you gave him, don't pay him a visit to urge him on or frighten him into the very actions that perpetuate those things for which humanity blames you. Let the pieces fall where they may."

"You know what Grams?" The Devil sighed as he leaned further back, the old woman's soothing touch on his brow, "I'm going to listen to you this time. I mean, how bad can it be?" The Devil stood up straight, nearly knocking his grandmother to the floor. He caught her with one hand and pointed to Heaven with the other. "I'm not taking the Jesus bait! Not ever again! You hear me?"

The Devil's grandmother hugged him. "It's okay, boy, it's okay."

The Devil looked down into his grandmother's eyes, "What if I hadn't Grams?" The Devil softened, his eyes pooled with tears, his blistered skin smoothed, he spoke, "What if I hadn't?"

Mitch Hudson was supposed to arrive by 7:30am for tee time at 8:00am on the one-hole golf course at Camp David. He was a no-show. Word was sent to Morty, who told the President, who was still upset because this was the one course he was able to beat most of his peers on.

The President, instead, began his day with the headlines and the sound of buses pulling up to his retreat house. Bethany McDonald poured him another cup of coffee as he put down the newspaper, then she poured one for herself. "Flora's going to be on one of those buses," she told Brian as he added sugar to her cup.

"How do you know?"

"Mother's intuition."

"You don't have mother's intuition."

"I know, Morty told me."

"Why didn't he tell me?"

"Flora told him not to."

"Why are you telling me then?"

"Flora doesn't tell me what to do."

Then both said, in unison, "yes she does." They laughed at first, then eased into awkward sighs as they realized, also in unison, that Flora had managed to win nearly every argument she had ever had with them and had gotten her way a good ninety percent of the time.

"Hi Mom, hi Daddy. I brought a few friends for breakfast." Behind Flora stood more black people than had ever been guests of Barack

Obama at Camp David, and Brian and Bethany watched more pour out of the second bus on their way to the breakfast table. There were a few white people along for the cause and one of them was Eli, whom the President singled out.

"Eli, Eli, it's good to see you," he forced a smile as he stood up to greet the crowd. His eyes fell upon Fitz who he thought he recognized but couldn't be sure because most young black men looked exactly the same to him, and he told himself that in his head as he considered whether to try to remember the young man's name or not. "A-a-n-n-d, Fritz?"

"Fitz, Mr. McPresident, I mean Mr. President." Fitz answered as if he had conflated Brian's surname with his title, when in fact, he intentionally defined the man standing in front of him as the corporate, capitalist, ruling class president of the privileged elite.

Brian McDonald extended his hand to Fitz and looked for a camera as he shook his hand. There were no cameras, and no one was recording. The President felt out of place.

"Why don't we all go where there's a little more room?" Bethany McDonald said as she demurely stood from the table.

Flora took pity on her mother and rounded up the troops, "Okay everyone, let's reassemble by the buses and talk about where we are all going to stay."

"Stay?" Bethany and Brian said in unison.

"Stay," replied Flora, Eli, Fitz, Ella, the entire body of both the Black Student Union and the LGBTQ union, accompanied by Black Lives Matter activists and three people who had no idea they were part of a protest but had heard that there were buses going to Camp David, in other words, cheap tourists. They began asking around if they could possibly get a ride home because they weren't planning on staying.

This was a logistic that Flora didn't want to mess around with, and Eli quickly advised them to simply ask the bus drivers if they could go back with them.

Brian put the notion of a fun morning of golf aside and began thinking about how he was going to keep himself from wringing his own daughter's neck. Flora was helping to organize campers, setting up tents like Camp David was a KOA. Morty had sent Bill and Amy over to protect the President but they surveyed the scene and determined the risk to be minimal. They ended up helping to set up most of the tents.

Morty brought a collapsible lounge chair for the President, every time he went to Camp David. Brian McDonald loved to be photographed, in a lounging position, enjoying a drink or a cigar, wherever and whenever he felt like it at Camp David. Morty had taken over three hundred "ad lib" photos and two dozen shots where the President wanted to be lounging in the same spot where other presidents had lounged or, even better, worked while at Camp David. It was important to President Brian McDonald to be the Best President, and that meant that he had to be the best at everything, including lounging and relaxing. It was in that moment of thought that Brian smelled the barbecue grills. Even before the tents were completely pitched, the grills were unpacked, assembled and loaded up with charcoal. This may have been one of the biggest groups to ever stay at Camp David, but this peaceful, activist delegation wasn't going to cost the taxpayers a dime. They came to stay, but they came prepared to take care of themselves.

"What the hell am I supposed to do now, Morty?" The President had never asked Morty what he was supposed to do about anything

Then again, he had never been in a gathering where he was a minority. Even when the President travelled to nations where the majority of citizens were people of color, he was backed by an army, so he wasn't afraid. Today he had Bill and Amy and they were helping the activists. "Go with it, Mr. President. Everyone loves a barbecue. We'll set up your chair and grab a few shots by the grills."

"I knew I kept you around for good reason." The President smiled and patted Morty on the back as he watched Bethany leave Camp David in his limousine. "Where's she off to?"

"I'll check with Bill," Morty responded quickly but received an expression of bewilderment from the President. "Redwood?"

"Yes, of course, I know his name," the President tried feebly to reinforce his story," Bill, my driver, he's a very good driver."

Bill Redford was more than the President's driver; he was one of two highly skilled security officers permanently assigned to his protection. Bill and Amy had devoted themselves to the security of the President and first lady from day one. From the moment Brian was inaugurated, Bill and Amy were on duty twenty-four-seven, three hundred and sixty-five days a year. They would only separate or leave the president's side if instructed to by the President himself or the first lady.

"The first lady sends her regrets but had to leave to make an appointment she nearly forgot." Morty relayed the words exactly as they were spoken into his earpiece. Those words had been relayed directly by Bill, who also knew that the first lady was lying.

"She's full of shit," Brian McDonald cupped his hand over his mouth in the direction of Morty, "she's just afraid of black people."

Morty knew that what the President said was true. "They're a major constituency, so she may as well learn to embrace them." Morty felt as though he may have just spoken his last words.

"What did you say?" The President was staring at a half of a chicken being turned over hot coals. He barely acknowledged that Morty had even spoken. He didn't look at black people as being like him, even when they enjoyed the same things he did. Flora would argue that he saw himself as above people of color and therefore, never considered them. At first, she thought it was just his thing. However, being exposed to vast numbers of people, as first daughter, she became increasingly aware that there were many different sorts of people who viewed other sorts of people as inferior for one reason or other. Somehow, despite being conditioned to share her father's narrow perspective, Flora viewed people as people. She had two rules that she lived by, but she couldn't tell you how she got there or where she heard them first. Rule number one, Peace first. She explained the rule to mean that peace was the goal, the primary objective and that it had several bullet points, the only kind of bullet she could stomach, the first of which was, "The primary objective cannot be achieved through conflict." Rule number two, "Live and let live." Flora would illustrate this rule in any number of ways, depending upon the situation or cause at hand.

"Foods!" Flora had developed a habit of yelling out "foods," whenever food was ready to be served, whether she did the cooking or not. She saw it as a way of celebrating the experience of dining. It was both an acknowledgement to the person who prepared the food and a battle cry. Flora took eating very seriously and never for a minute lacked appreciation for the fact that she had something to eat. That infectious energy spread through the encampment until the President opened his big mouth.

"I just want to say a few words before we all eat." Brian McDonald looked around. No one was paying any attention to him. They were all getting their food and enjoying the music. He looked at Morty, pointed to the DJ, then ran a finger under his own throat. Morty's eyes found Amy's. He pointed to his own ear, pointed to the DJ and slowly lowered his hand palm flat, and before his motion had ended the music was turned down. "I am so happy you all decided to join me on my vacation," the President lied, "and I'm proud to give you people an opportunity to celebrate your culture. And I want to tell you that you all matter. Everybody Matters!"

The music went from turned down, to turned off. If a crowd could ever share a single face, that time was now, and that face said, "What-the-fuck?"

Some of the more optimistic members of the crowd had convinced themselves that they were going to gain some ground in the battle for racial equality, simply because they had not been asked to leave. They saw it as a sign that the President respected them and was prepared to listen to their grievances. Flora knew her mother would flee but had never imagined that her father would say something so devoid of understanding. She had no delusions that her father viewed people of color as equals, and that was why she brought everyone to Camp David to confront him, but she thought she would have more time to create an atmosphere where he might see and feel how truly equal all of humanity is. The only thing that went wrong in her plan was believing that her father would ever even try to change his own views.

"You!" Flora yelled in the direction of Brian. She was carrying a plate, loaded with a half-chicken, coleslaw, two ears of buttered corn-on-the-cob and beans. "Go back inside. You aren't getting any of this food, dad. You don't deserve it."

No one was moving. Even the children who had been running around playing were standing and looking at the President to see what he would do. The entire nation knew that Flora didn't refer to her father as anything but daddy unless she was thoroughly pissed. Even when she was pissed, she would mostly say "daddy," in a very snotty way. There was that fact and the other perhaps more important one, that he was the president, and she was his daughter.

"Yeah?" McDonald turned his back on his daughter and waved his hand dismissively in the air as he walked away, "well, you and all of your friends can just finish up your little picnic and get the hell off my lawn."

Chapter 17

Things went from bad to worse for the people of the United States, while the military increased its stronghold on other nations and the country continued to conduct foreign policy by brute force.

Eli, Flora, Ella and Fitz all continued what they had started at Camp David and pulled in the disenfranchised to a cause they had no idea how to define. Black Lives Matter leaders met regularly with them to ensure that their own message was not lost in the rising tide of followers to the unnamed movement they now found themselves spearheading.

"Classless Co-op!" Fitz blurted out, then turned his eyeballs violently toward his own brain as everyone laughed at his suggestion.

"We don't have to worry about a name," Eli posited, "the media will put a name to this as soon as they recognize this as Occupy and BLM joining forces with whatever it is we have managed to scrape together here at school."

"I don't think we should leave it to them," Ella stood up from her lotus position on the floor with an ease that made it seem as though she could defy gravity at will. "I'm not a big fan of the corporate media and I don't want them putting a name on my passion." Everyone agreed. "I'm not saying this is the greatest name, but I think it works," Ella paused expecting a reaction, preparing her defense, "HOMO." Ella looked at Flora, Fitz and Eli. None of them said anything but all were staring directly into her eyes, no matter which one she looked at, as if they were waiting for something else. They all looked at one another. They all looked back at Ella. They all laughed.

"Homo, seriously?" Fitz was smiling, his eyes soft with pity.

"Yes, seriously," Ella replied, mimicking his expression. She looked at each person in turn as she explained, "HOMO, all in capital letters." Ella saw three faces with the exact same expression staring back at her. There were no words. "Okay, let me explain it." She stood with her feet apart and planted firmly. "It comes from homo sapiens and it's everything we have been talking about." Ella was looking at three very smart people and each of them was giving her the same stupid face. She decided to attempt to articulate the message of their movement, since they hadn't really planned on starting one. "WE ARE HOMO," Ella cried, her hands pressed up against the sky, or in this case the ceiling in Eli and Flora's Boston penthouse. "EVERYBODY IS HOMO," her hands pumped the sky, evangelical preacher style, "and together, we defeat the machine. Because the machine is NOT HOMO. The machine is corruption. The machine is opulence. The machine is greed. The machine will crush the body, but it cannot crush HOMO. We the species, in order to create a more perfect union, do stand against the machine. We stand against COG, Corruption Opulence Greed." All eyes were glued to Ella and she felt an uncontrollable urge, "Can I get an Amen?"

"Amen." The group responded, each with a different intonation. Fitz gave Ella "WTF" face because Ella didn't have a habit of speaking like a Baptist preacher and he had never actually seen her pray. Flora was truly caught up in Ella's passion and responded with a heartfelt amen, whereas Eli thought about the Devil. They hadn't mentioned the Devil to anyone since hiding within his grandmother's hair because they didn't see how it would change anything. It was all a bit much to consider, and it had been since it happened, but now, just as then, more pressing matters were at hand.

"Ella, I love that COG thing you said, Corruption Opulence Greed, it's exactly what's wrong with our society," Eli always evaluated how the consumer of the information might perceive it and that was part of their success as a YouTube celebrity, "but don't you think that some people who might agree with our cause would be put off by the associations with the word HOMO?"

"Well, that's just it, isn't it, Eli?" Ella was on a roll, "We need to change the association. It isn't as though we haven't done it before. For example, the word queer, once a slur, now a banner. Gay, what about gay?" Ella was becoming even more attached to her semi-impulsive proposal to use the word HOMO to define their movement. "We can own HOMO and make it a word we are proud of like never before!"

"I gotta go with Ella on this one, Eli." Flora stood up and performed a little forearm bump, followed by a hip bump with Ella. "If someone won't join us because we call ourselves HOMO, they don't get it to begin with. It's sorta the best litmus test we could have without subjecting people to an actual test. And I'm not saying that there aren't any homosexuals out there who are against us, just not nearly as many as there are heterosexuals who find themselves in opposition to the unified causes we are fighting for. Count me in Ella, We Are HOMO!"

Eli and Fitz looked to one another, smiled, and raised their fists in the air as well, "We Are HOMO!"

"We are HOMO, dun d-dun d-dun d-DUN!" Fitz sang to the tune of the Farmers Insurance jingle then laughed at his own joke. Everyone laughed and each of them felt the need to sing the freshly bastardized jingle repeatedly. They continued singing and laughing at the jingle for several minutes, each spinning it toward their own expression. Fitz went beyond in his rendition, rubbing his black skin as if he represented all black people everywhere, while Ella accentuated the curves of her body as she danced to represent women, while Flora swept up a small pot of herbs she was growing in her penthouse window and held it aloft.

"Hold on," Eli interrupted her dance, "what exactly does the pot symbolize?"

Flora looked slightly miffed, "really Eli?" She swept the fragrant rosemary and basil under their nose as she continued her dance. "My plants represent the environment, family farming and sustainability, silly."

Eli did feel silly because that should have been immediately apparent to them. Eli was just having a moment. That moment lasted for two, then they snapped out of it, quite literally. Eli snapped their fingers and threw their right hand up in the air and their left pointed at their knee, looking like a cross between a bullfighter and a flamenco dancer. They tapped their feet and moved fluidly toward Flora. The raised right hand fell to Flora's hips while the left took the potted plant from her hands and laid it back in its place of origin within a single motion. Eli moved Flora around the living room with grace and strength, then pulled her down on top of them onto the couch. "Can you guess what this represents?" Eli cooed as they kissed Flora.

"Your right to be sexy?" She remained on top of them, kissing and rolling deeper into the embrace.

"Well, okay," Fitz said as he looked at Ella who was smiling back at him. "Normally, I'd say something along the lines of, get a room, but this is your place and, well, technically this is your room." Ella was still smiling at him and Eli and Flora were busy sorting out which tongue belonged to whom. Fitz was a smart man and didn't need to be led around like a dog, most of the time.

"C'mon baby," Ella said softly as she held a hand out to Fitz. She led him down the hall of the penthouse to a guest room they had stayed in many times before.

The meeting had fallen apart, but it had done so in the best way possible. The four leaders of the movement spent the next couple of hours thinking only of each other. Later, when they assembled with other movement leaders, from groups with differing goals, they brought up Ella's idea. The debate and discussion that erupted over using the word HOMO to represent their movement proved its worthiness. Everyone agreed that it was the perfect way to get eyeballs on their movement.

The decision to embrace HOMO did not go over well with a great many members within the various groups and causes. However, the talking heads on the news couldn't get enough of it and eventually, recognizing the opportunity to voice their objectives, those group members came around. Before anyone knew what hit them, members of groups who felt they had nothing in common with those of other groups began to discover common ground. The more these groups got together, the more similarities they discovered. In each case, the enemy was not clearly identifiable. It was impossible to nail down where things went wrong because there was just so much of it. The young leaders who were spearheading the movement were not raised to be leaders in many cases; they became leaders out of necessity. Flora and Eli were rare commodities within their circle of friends and fellow activists. They were expected to be leaders, Flora out of association with her father, and Eli out of celebrity.

The talking heads, controlled by the mass media, corporate elite, only wanted to talk to Eli and Flora. Black Lives Matter leaders, activists for the environment, indigenous leaders, LGBTQ activists were completely overlooked as networks scrambled to get interviews with Flora and Eli. They turned down all interviews, which infuriated the media. When confronted on the street and asked to comment on the Black Lives Matter movement, Eli told reporters to ask Alicia Garza.

When Flora was stopped by reporters on her way into the grocery store to express her views on the same topic, she asked for a moment and walked across the parking lot, out of view of the cameras. When she came back around the corner, Flora was walking with a young woman of color. She walked through the group of reporters and cameras, "I'm not really qualified to comment, but I found someone who is, for you to talk to." Flora smiled as she placed a palm on the young woman's shoulder. "Her name is Susan. I just met her, and you know what, she has something to say about the Black Lives Matter movement." Flora scooted off quickly into the store leaving the reporters and cameras with a real person of color, Susan, willing to talk about her own life as a black woman in America. Not a single one of the reporters had the courage to go off script to interview Susan.

The media had to find another way to talk about the issues. They had become accustomed to people who wanted to be on the news. Flora and Eli had decided that they would not be the voices of the movement no matter what it became. Instead, they elevated cause leaders who had been ignored. As HOMO, groups that had been fighting separately banded together. HOMO never made any statement other than "We Are HOMO," and at every rally, every meeting, the core of what transpired came from the groups who collectively comprised HOMO. So, whenever the media went to cover a HOMO event, they would be confronted by climate activists, LGBTQ activists, Black Lives Matter activists, leaders from White Earth Nation and other indigenous tribes and communities, instead of a single cause. This gave the media no way to prepare, no way to craft their soundbites. They were confronted by and at the mercy of the truth. When all voices were heard, none could be silenced and inevitably, the media had no choice but to report on what was happening all around them. The people were taking the country back, and the people were guiding the narrative.

Chapter 18

HOMO swept the nation. With the combined buying power of women, people of color environmental activists, LGBTQ activists and the sixty-plus percent of white men polled, HOMO was reported as the greatest influence in the market. Corporations and their executives were now crying out for the very lifeblood of the corporate body, revenue, and HOMO was thrifty. Through a great amount of effort and community involvement, people were able to eat less expensively, commute responsibly, and leave jobs that only served to widen the gap between those who owned and those who served. The big-box, chain stores that had replaced so many small-town businesses began to dry up because the people learned together that community health doesn't come from convincing advertisements and slashed prices. People began to understand where and how big business had assumed control of their lives, and together, they forged a solution.

Eli, Flora, Ella and Fitz faded into the background as the leaders who had shaped movements, staged protests and worked to educate the people were heard, not just by members of their own coalitions but by those fighting to combat other injustices and consequences of corporate greed. For the first time, the leaders of more than eighty percent of activist organizations assembled in one room to have a town hall style meeting where they could express their frustrations and offer their solutions. They found that they shared more than they didn't and that the disparity between them, if any, generally arose from the very system that oppressed them. No one argued that racism did not exist in America. Flora, who organized the meeting, with the help of roughly one hundred co-activists, helped to write the guidelines for the meeting which stated that certain conditions must be agreed to by all parties before any real discussion could take place.

Jasmine Peters, a black woman who lost her leg to a bomb planted by a white nationalist at a Black Lives Matter rally, began the meeting, "We Are HOMO an--"

"WE ARE HOMO!" The group chanted back before she could finish. "WE ARE HOMO, WE ARE HOMO, they repeated until Jasmine raised her hand and lowered it slowly.

"Thank you, thank you, thank you," Jasmine said as the large group became quiet. "I am here to read the rules of this meeting, but I can see that you all are my people, so this isn't really gonna be necessary." She smiled as a laugh of acknowledgement rolled its way across the meeting hall. "But let's do this anyway, just in case some of you want or need to hear it." Jasmine was a strong speaker and an even stronger woman, "Racism is real!" The group cheered an awkward mix of affirmations, hoots and handclaps. "Climate Change is real!" The group began to catch on that a cheer represented an acknowledgement of the fact and not support for its existence, and they responded a bit more enthusiastically. "People are allowed to be who they are and love who they love!" The cheering swelled even louder so Jasmine decided to bring it back around, "all right then, let's hear it one more time for Black Lives Matter!"

"Black Lives Matter, Black Lives Matter, Black Lives Matter," the group was now standing.

Jasmine took the microphone from the stand in one hand and stepped out from behind the podium. With her other hand she raised her crutch that now served as her right leg. She had no prosthetic limb because she had no insurance. She had no insurance because she had no job. She had no job because she had owned a hardware store in a small town and developers came in and bought the next town over. They put in a big-box chain grocery store, restaurants, a movie theater and a giant church. They also put in an immense hardware store. They had done their research and they figured out the best land to buy in order to get the most traffic from the surrounding suburbs and towns while remaining close enough to the city to draw a bit of traffic from there as well. In this way, they could avoid buying out competing businesses and instead, they could simply loss-leader the surrounding small businesses out of existence. Jasmine stood on one leg, crutch high in the air, "WE ARE HOMO!"

"WE ARE HOMO! WE ARE HOMO! WE ARE HOMO!" The meeting had begun.

The meeting lasted for five days, and in that time, the leaders compared solutions. They discovered that they had become leaders for many of the same reasons, life had forced it upon them. They had felt the urge to contribute, not for personal gain but out of a need to see justice, reason, and unity restored. Society had been manipulated by a system run amuck. Capitalism, purely for the sake of Capitalism had become the rule of law, and most of the institutions from academic to religious were complicit.

Extricating themselves from the web that society had entrapped them in was the goal. Recognizing their own contributions to that entanglement was the challenge. While Eli had intentionally assumed the role of reporter for the movement, their visibility enhanced that of the movement and Eli became even more of a celebrity. This made it difficult to fade from media attention until Fitz came up with a suggestion. "Why don't we all just quit watching TV?"

"We don't watch TV," Ella quickly responded as if the mere mention of television was distasteful.

"Game of Thrones."

"That's HBO, that doesn't count."

"Yes, it does."

"Well, there aren't any new ones now anyway, so I can just stop completely."

"What about football?"

"What about football?"

"That's TV."

"No, it isn..." Ella sighed in deep frustration. "Yes, it is," she acknowledged. "I really do watch TV."

"Y'know, I do too," Flora admitted. "I watch television for the news, even though I know it's coming directly from daddy. Well, daddy and the men who tell daddy what to do."

"Damn, that's a mouthful," Fitz laughed, "I don't even want to begin parsing that one out!"

"I agree," Eli chimed in, "I think we all should just stop watching TV. In fact, I propose we stop consumption of everything corporate."

"Everything?" Ella held up her Starbucks cup.

"Everything."

And that's just what they did. They got thirty-eight percent of the population to stop shopping, going to work and using television or internet in any way.

Because they had done it, they missed four big story news cycles which ended up condensing down to only two minutes of explanation when people who had consumed the media tried to explain it to those who hadn't. Many of those who had not gone to work out of protest were fired, a large percentage of whom realized shortly thereafter that the job they had was easily replaceable. Those who meant something to the company, business or organization they worked for were welcomed back into the office or workplace. They were more important than the position itself.

Those who had shopped ahead in planning for the two weeks found that they didn't use as much food or toilet paper as they had planned and that they actually consumed far less than they had thought they might need. In fact, the net result was that people bought substantially less after they had gone through some sort of self-imposed limitations. They simply didn't need everything they had grown accustomed to. For many, it became the difference between being a slave to the system and developing their own. This change affected the economic well-being of the country in a way that few had anticipated - it changed the individuals' economic situation rather than that of the large corporations which had seen a dramatic drop in profit. Restaurants, coffee shops and grocery stores all saw a dramatic decline in sales but a large percentage of those, predominantly family-owned businesses, had closed in support of HOMO.

Ironically, the news story that had the longest run and continued throughout the COG Buster Boycott, a name Fitz came up with that finally stuck, was the boycott itself. People who had not observed the boycott flooded coworkers who had with questions about what it was like, how terrible it might have been, and how could they do that to the company and themselves. Inevitably, those questioned would ask how things had been in their absence, only to learn, almost invariably, that not much of anything had changed. What had changed was most often a decline in urgency. Coworkers cited numerous instances where the company advised against moving forward on initiatives that were in the mix until extenuating circumstances could be resolved.

"So, what have we learned?" Mitch Hudson asked the President over a burger at the titty bar.

"Mwuffin," Brian McDonald responded through the chewed meat, cheese and saliva-soaked bread that blocked the efforts of his larynx. He swallowed as Mitch knocked back another whiskey, on America's tab. "Nothing," the President managed as he wiped his face with a napkin that had a woman's shapely leg printed on one side and reflected on the other. It was printed that way so that you might have your face inside the woman's crotch as you cleaned yourself. The person sitting across from you as you wiped would enjoy the view of you diving in as well, your hands pressing into her splayed legs as you used her to clear away the aftermath of your insatiable hunger. At least that's what the graphic artist told the bar management when he came up with the design. They ate it up. "Nothing at all! I am not doing anything for Flora ever again in her life!" Brian McDonald nearly choked on what was left in his throat when he began shouting. Mitch Hudson motioned for two more whiskeys. He then motioned for another two for the President.

"You've been a good father." Mitch spoke calmly as he leaned in close to the President, "kids will be kids, Bri. You've got a whole world that looks up to you. She'll come around." Hudson leaned back and spoke loudly enough for several tables around to hear him, "So, what are you going to do about HOMO?"

"The whole thing's over, Mitch. There's nothing I can do about it."
Brian McDonald knocked back both whiskeys and motioned for two
more.

"Brian, it isn't over." Mitch slammed his whiskeys with equal fervor
to the President, "they have just started, and they are going to keep
at it until you stop them."

"Well, I can't." The President drained another whiskey.

"M-m-m, yes, you can." Mitch Hudson kept step with the President
on the whiskey.

"There you go again Mitch! You want me to impose martial law."
The President lowered his voice, "We agreed that martial law is a
last resort. The American people will not stand for it."

"Unless there's a pandemic." Hudson spoke as though he had a
pandemic in his pocket.

"That's murder."

"Is it?"

"Yes, Mitch," Brian became very still. "Releasing a virus that you
know will kill old people everywhere is murder."

"Well, it doesn't have to just be old people."

"What are you saying Mitch?"

"You wouldn't be doing anything unnatural, that's why it's called
"Natural Selection.""

"Hold on, Mitch. What you are talking about is genocide."

"No, Brian," Hudson explained, "if you were capable of genocide,
your troubles with HOMO would be over. No, unfortunately, you'll
have to lose a few of your own in the process. This is more of a

paring down than a weeding out. That's where the martial law comes in. The virus is just so you get full support for the martial law."

Brian felt a sense of illness wash over him.

"But don't worry, Bri," Mitch Hudson spoke so smoothly, it made Brian feel warm inside, "we've got you and your entire family covered, including Flora."

"Whaddya' mean?"

"Don't go stupid on me, McDonald." Hudson knocked back another whiskey and looked at the President's glass. Brian slammed his whiskey down. "You know we've been working on these viruses for decades, Mitch burped, "And, there's a vaccine."

Brian McDonald wasn't sure how to feel. He had become comfortable with a lot of responsibility and decision making throughout his career and his presidency, but this one seemed like more of a burden. Flora's decision to work against him by embracing the people rather than the cozy world of corporate domination he had built her was taking its toll on his emotions, of which he admittedly had few remaining. Of those that did linger around the remnants of his heart, his love for Flora was the hardest to let go. Despite their quarrels, he would never want anything bad to happen to his daughter and being assured that she would survive made the decision possible.

"Let's do it."

Chapter 19

The disease started in China, in a street market. From there, it spread across the world.

It destroyed the HOMO movement. A movement that was people-based and community centered, driven by human interaction. That very same movement became a threat as human interaction led to the spread of the virus. Even its own leaders had to appeal to the people to remain indoors, wear masks and endure the loss of loved ones in the wait for the vaccine.

Flora and Eli counted themselves lucky that they were together and could remain safe. Oddly, Flora became homesick for the White House. Eli, who had always had a good relationship with their parents, missed them even more but acknowledged that the practice of social distancing was important in preventing the spread of the virus. They were unable to see their friends because the President ordered an immediate lockdown to address the virus.

The virus had changed everything. The people had given up on HOMO and, by extension, all that had made the movement successful, for the limited time people had been allowed to assemble, in America, to voice their belief in equality and social justice.

Brian McDonald was not an idiot. He saw how the people still cared for one another, despite the lack of access to one another. Mitch Hudson had been right when he suggested that people would still help one another, even if they felt threatened and that the only way to get them all to stay away from each other was to inflate the death toll. The President already owned one of the major media networks, while Hudson owned two. The remaining three were held by other individuals who were more than willing to enable the President in his mission to highlight the urgency of a strict, "Stay in Place," message, bolstered by the constant reporting of the death toll with little to no research into the total numbers of cases. This gap in reporting was explained by describing the virus as unusual and hard to test for, particularly because the virus shared so many symptoms with the flu.

People began watching one another. Neighborhood social media sites were riddled then bombarded with posts where one neighbor would blame another for exposing them to the virus while at the grocery store or when out for a walk. Suddenly, friends turned on friends as the fight over wearing masks escalated to absurdity. There was no argument that people were getting sick from the virus. Nearly half of the country believed they wouldn't contract the virus and that even if they did, they would be fine. The other half of the country believed that the virus was deadly and that it was their social responsibility to wear a mask to protect others. Brian McDonald pulled the trigger when he reached the fifty-fifty split, it was all he needed to impose martial law, in order to get the fifty percent who would not wear masks to wear them, or at least, to make them stay inside.

Americans united behind President Brian McDonald, who after tragically contracting the virus, while on the front lines in his fight to beat the virus, assured them that he would, "get through this!" The President was assured by Mitch Hudson that the serum he had agreed to ingest, was not the virus but a strain concocted to resemble the virus, which wasn't really important because they had a vaccine. He believed Mitch and trusted Mitch because Mitch always seemed to want what he wanted.

Brian McDonald recovered quickly from the virus, cementing himself in the hearts of the nation as a hero. "I will take what I have learned, what we all have learned, what science has learned, and I will deliver a vaccine!"

Even though he knew that there was a vaccine, Brian McDonald was terrified of the virus because people were really dying. He didn't want it to reach Flora before he did, so, he flew to Boston, during lockdown, in the midst of martial law, to bring her the vaccine, ahead of schedule. Everyone, inside and outside, everywhere he looked was wearing a mask. His quick imposition of martial law had garnered an impressive fifty-seven percent approval rating. The airports were all but empty and there was much confusion over what defined non-essential personnel, but his plan was working. Brian couldn't remember if it was his plan or if Mitch came up with it, but he was so invigorated by his approval rating that he completely forgot that he had released a virus. As he entered Flora's apartment to offer her the vaccine, he felt noble, rather than diabolical.

"What do you mean you have a vaccine?" Flora had been blindsided by the virus, just like everyone else. She had no idea that it was manufactured by Hudson and his secret service cronies and released by her own father, Hudson was an equal opportunity meddler and warmonger. He made sure the virus was going to happen one way or another and planned to capitalize on it. Brian, and a half-dozen other leaders of nations were trying to get their families to take the vaccine at precisely the same time. Flora's questions over the vaccine were echoed across those nations. "How do you know it works?"

"It's been thoroughly tested."

"By whom?"

"We've got people on it," Brian realized he was talking to his daughter and not the average member of the American public.

"Scientists and doctors from both the military and commercial sectors have assured me that it is safe and effective." Brian pulled a thumb drive from his pocket and held it out to Flora, "it's all on this thumb drive."

"Well, I'm sure there are a lot of people who are more at risk than I am." Flora was wrestling with her own inner turmoil over her feelings for her father and her sense of what was right for the American people. If her daddy's administration actually had developed a vaccine, it was good news for the world. "Thank you, daddy." Flora looked at Brian with all the love she could muster, which wasn't much after Camp David. "What about mom?"

"She's stranded in Saint-Tropez, but we've got people there. She'll be alright." The President motioned to the White House staff medical assistant, Mary, who was standing by, staring at Flora. To Mary, it was like being in the presence of a movie star. Mary was six years older than Flora but idolized her just the same. Mary stepped toward Flora.

"No thanks, Mary." Flora said gratefully. Mary eyes, above her mask, clearly indicated she was crestfallen. "Look, daddy," Flora was a very loving person and despite being beyond angry with her father over Camp David, she loved him, "I am not getting a vaccine until those who need it most have gotten theirs." She was doing her best to not escalate the situation to a political debate but couldn't help herself, "what are you going to do about people who don't have insurance?"

"We're making more all the time," Brian smiled as he held his hand out toward Mary, "now, just let the girl do her job." Mary smiled at Flora through the President's insult.

"Wow, dad, just wow!"

"There it is again. You can't accept anything from me. I always have to be on the other side. Ever since the straws!" The President threw up his hands in frustration as Eli entered the room from the hallway, their pajamas enhanced if not arguably "completed" by a stocking cap, hand-knitted by Flora. "And there he, it, they is, are," the President fell apart over Eli's identity at times of stress, "the very reason I don't have a relationship with my daughter."

Eli was still a bit sleepy and had only come out to say hello. Eli decided to abort that mission and turned around and went back to their room, leaving the President with nowhere to point his anger, other than Mary, who was still holding her medical kit slightly aloft.

"Put that down," the President cried, "can't you see nobody wants my vaccine?"

Flora smiled at Amy and Morty as Brian McDonald continued to hang his head. They all knew when to be silent in the presence of the President except for poor Mary.

"It won't hurt at all," she offered sweetly to Flora.

"Put it down and get out!" The President pointed to the door with his gaze still directed straight at the floor. He raised his eyes and looked at Mary, frightening her with a scowl she had not seen on the President's face before. Amy and Morty had seen it and were not surprised when it circled their way. They left the penthouse and stood in awkward silence in the hall.

The President opened the door and put just his head out into the hall. "Wait in the limo."

"But Mr. President, I..." Amy was cut short by her boss.

"There's no one in the hotel and I have imposed martial law." Brian's face became even more stern, "I don't even need you at all right now. Nobody's going to get to me. Nobody's allowed on the damn street! Now go."

Morty and Amy were good friends with Flora. They hadn't seen her since the virus first hit and they missed her. The President had robbed them of any opportunity to even speak with her. They had no clue that the President was involved in spreading the virus. If they had, both would have left their positions in the White House. They first thought about leaving after Camp David. They hadn't been able to see how deeply racist and selfishly elitist the President truly was until that day. Flora talked both of them into staying on with her father. Leaving the penthouse without a chance to talk was hard on them. Morty had to pull Amy all the way into the elevator before the doors closed.

Mary was standing in Emerson's spot and he could feel her sadness. He was thankful that he wasn't there for any of them. He had had a very unique perspective on life and death in the Ames Hotel and thought that he might write a novel about it one day. Emerson remembered what Eli had told him about handing over the key to the elevator. He had been biding his time, waiting for the moment when one of those who were passing on might intentionally turn his key, relieving him of his duty as elevator operator to the Devil. He fantasized about how it might occur, but all of his fantasies came up dry. He could imagine no situation in which a passenger to Hell might want to take his job. There had been many who had tried to take the key from him. They were all trying to stop the elevator. Emerson could sense that reason. A much different passage to Hell consumed those who shared that reason, literally. Emerson would transform into a magnificent beast and devour the passenger, generally starting small with the extremities. He could never slow himself down enough to really savor the experience. He regretted that in times of passenger compliance, which was the norm.

The elevator reached the lobby and Mary pressed the door open button, a habit she had on all elevators. Mary had the notion that elevators always wanted to be closed and that they worked at being that way unless you held down the door open button. She had never been willing to explore the possibility of anything different, so she always positioned herself at the button panel of an elevator. Amy stepped off the elevator first. Morty held a hand toward the door and said, "go ahead." He hadn't noticed how Mary had ushered the elevator to the penthouse upon their arrival because the President was talking his ear off about his approval rating.

"I like to get off last," Mary offered demurely and Morty stepped off. She let go of the button and hopped to the floor outside in a single bound.

Meanwhile in the penthouse, the President's eyes were full of tears as he stood up. "I need you to take this vaccine, Flora."

"I don't need it as much as others, and why do I get it before everyone else?"

"Look, the fact of the matter is, I'm going to make the announcement today." The President hadn't planned to announce the vaccine for a couple of weeks. The idea was to ride his recovery numbers and announce the vaccine if they dipped. That was still the plan.

"Promise?"

"I promise."

"A Daddy Promise?"

Brian McDonald was a liar and a cheat and a snob and a bully to anyone whenever he needed to be. He just had a masterful way of disguising it. There was only one person he couldn't boldface lie to.

The only thing she could truly count on from Brian, however, was a Daddy Promise. He knew if he made the promise, he would have to keep it. He didn't have time to consult with Mitch and he felt scared. "A Daddy Promise."

"Okay, I'll get Eli while you get Mary back up here."

"It's just one injection." The President answered without thinking.

"One?" Flora was stunned. "Wait a second. You flew all the way here, on the day you are going to announce to the world that you have a vaccine, to deliver one to me first. And nothing for Eli." Suddenly a rush of apprehension overtook her, "Hold on. Why would you even do that? If you have millions of vials of vaccines ready to go, why on earth would you only bring one?"

Brian McDonald was silent. Flora knew it as the kind of guilty that he was incapable of explaining. She had seen him like this before. If he was guilty with an explanation, his mouth usually moved around considerably to form words to obscure the guilt.

"You don't really have a vaccine, do you?"

"No. Well, I mean yes. We have a vaccine." Brian knew he had to come forward with some small percentage of the truth to satisfy Flora. "I just can't announce it yet."

"But you made a Daddy Promise."

"Yes, I did. And I'm sorry. I lied."

"On a Daddy Promise! You lied on a Daddy Promise!"

"I did it to protect you."

"Protect me? I don't need your protection. You got sick and got better and I'm in a lot better shape than you are." Flora had had it with her father. "Get out and take your one little vaccine with you,

you petty, selfish..." Flora disintegrated into tears and pointed to the door.

The President hung his head. He reached for the bag, then left it instead. He didn't say a word as he left the only person who was important to him, sobbing over disappointment in him. His ears began to ring as he waited for the elevator. The skin across his back felt tight as he stepped inside. He felt anxious, alone and angry with himself and Mitch Hudson.

"Going down?" Emerson asked from the corner of the elevator as he closed the doors.

The President had never noticed that there was an elevator operator before. He hadn't noticed that the elevator operator was dressed in clothing from another time. He began to wonder if the whole hotel was period themed and he just hadn't noticed.

"Of course I'm going down." Brian McDonald looked at Emerson with disdain. He wanted to get down quickly and he was annoyed by Emerson. He wanted to see Mitch Hudson, so he could yell at him for his terrible idea. "I don't have a lot of time." Brian McDonald stared at the buttons on the elevator panel. They appeared older than he had remembered them, and there lodged in the keyhole, at the bottom of the panel, was a key, with a dog whistle keychain hanging from it.

"So, you're ready to go?" Emerson asked Brian.

"Yes, yes, of course I am." Brian McDonald was becoming even more impatient.

"Okay, I just wanted to be sure you wanted to go down," Emerson confirmed.

"Look, I don't know what you're doing, but I need to go now!" The President was not accustomed to waiting, especially after he had given an order.

"Just one more time, to be clear, you want to go."

"If I have to tell you one more time."

"Okay, okay," Emerson teased, "just wanted to know who was so important that the President of the United States was in such a hurry to see when his wonderful daughter was just in the other room. Your wife no doubt."

Brian McDonald was now furious with Emerson and therefor blurted out irrationally, "No, it isn't my wife, you idiot, it's fucking Mitch Hudson!"

"Okay, great, so, the Devil himself?"

"Wait," Brian McDonald was sweating profusely, "you know Mitch Hudson?"

"Everybody does," Emerson replied, making no effort to press any buttons, which further infuriated McDonald.

'Get the fuck out of my way you little piece of shit!" Brian McDonald slammed Emerson into the corner of the elevator and grabbed a hold of the keys. He turned them as he pressed the down button repeatedly, squashing Emerson up against the wall even further.

"My pleasure," Emerson responded as he disappeared.

Ding!

The President was all alone in the elevator.

The doors did not open. The elevator music had changed to his favorite tune, which eased him a bit. Little did he know that it would soon become his least favorite. His purpose returned and he hit the "door open" button hard. The doors opened and Brian McDonald was stunned.

He saw a vast chamber before him, a wide staircase leading down from a balcony just outside the elevator. The appearance of the elevator had changed, the President finally noticed, to luxurious and ornate, with a hint of gaudy. He stood frozen in the elevator doorway, unable to step further, his footfall not even complete. Just the tip of his left foot was touching the floor of the elevator behind him. His right foot was stuck, high in mid-step. Even his tiny, little nose felt squashed by the air in front of him, and in that instant, he saw him. The face of Mitch Hudson stepped its way closer to the top of the staircase, followed by his impeccably attired body.

"Hey Bri," Hudson smiled warmly, "You're early." He walked closer to Brian who was still transfixed between the elevator and gravity. "And, another surprise, you have already assumed a new career." Hudson walked past the President and into the elevator. As he did, Brian McDonald turned in his direction and to his great relief discovered that he was able to step back into the elevator.

"What the hell is going on here Mitch?" Brian yelled so loudly it reverberated throughout the old elevator causing the metal ring on the end of the elevator key to sway back and forth. The dog whistle was no longer attached to the ring. When Brian looked back at Hudson, his face had changed along with his hair color. The impeccable dress remained.

"A perfect choice of words Mr. President," the Devil grinned, "but I'm afraid you're just Brian now." The Devil's expression changed from amused to disappointed, "y'know, the thing is Bri, you kinda fucked me over, and I don't like that."

Brian McDonald felt ill. He recognized the Devil, but he had convinced himself that his previous encounter was a hallucination. Now that he was standing in the same elevator as the Devil and the former Mitch Hudson, everything made sense. A very horrible sense it was, but everything did fall together neatly into a life that had been manipulated by the Devil. It was his life, but he had allowed it to be guided by the Devil himself and rather than throw up on him, Brian McDonald ran headlong toward the staircase. He didn't make it out of the elevator. Even though the doors had remained open, it was as though they hadn't. Brian hit something and it hurt. He fell onto the floor of the elevator and found himself looking at the Devil's slick leather shoes. He turned his head upward to look at the Devil and watched as the Devil morphed from a human form to that of a horrible beast. It was far more terrifying than any beast Brian had ever imagined, and he found himself floating in an oil-like blackness of searing pain. The Devil's face had become truly demonic and his very expression intensified Brian's pain. Brian's father had suffered from gout. He had seen his father's inflated feet, red with swelling and sores, and remembered him saying how his only hope was that Brian would never feel such pain. He hadn't appreciated those words until this moment. Brian thought there could never be such pain as he was now feeling, until the Devil spoke.

"You are early!" The Devil screamed like a million witches, howled with the voice of every wolf that had ever lived and died, all through some kind of noise that wasn't so much sound as pain itself. "I had plans for you." Brian felt each cell of his brain being pulled apart from the others. The pain spread with each word the Devil said. "Your path was clear. You had everything in place because I gave you everything." The Devil was furious, he had melted everything in sight. There were no longer any walls to the elevator. There was no elevator, only pain and intense heat, intense cold, constant nausea, deafening sounds, blinding light and perpetual darkness, all experienced simultaneously, and then it stopped.

"I told you he'd go early." The Devil's grandmother was standing just outside the elevator door. "I win." Brian McDonald recognized the old woman, despite the change in her appearance. She was quite radiant and wasn't dressed at all like the day he had met her.

"Willow Breckburn?" Brian was still reeling from the pain of having his entire body disintegrated then suddenly snapped back together. "How?"

"See there, my little Lucy?" Willow teased the Devil, "dumb as a stump."

The Devil looked a little exhausted from his outburst but slicked himself up quickly, using his own hands as a sort of buffing device. Brian felt the pain leave his body and felt remarkably at ease given the circumstances. "It's only 'cause she's here," the Devil scowled at Brian, "I'm not finished with you." The Devil turned to Willow, "you still didn't win."

"It's not over," Willow replied as she stood in the doorway of the elevator, "and really, Lucifer, I'm only here for the job description."

"But I'm not finished with him," Lucifer pouted.

"I know, I know," his grandmother consoled him, "but there's new arrivals coming in twelve minutes, so I'd best get on with it. Now, run along and melt something. Oh, I almost forgot, I put some fresh beans in the grinder if you wouldn't mind brewing up a little coffee.

After all, you weren't the only one surprised by this jackass showing up now. And frankly, I'm going to miss Emerson."

"I don't often notice the help," the Devil said as he stepped off the elevator, "but, he was a good one." The Devil turned back and smiled at his grandmother, "he was so good at grabbing their coffee before they had a chance to sip it."

"He really shouldn't have been here in the first place," his grandmother added, "unlike this one. Speaking of which, I'd better get on with it." The Devil walked away to make coffee and Willow turned to face Brian. "You're dead."

Brian looked at her, then looked in the direction the Devil had gone, then looked at the elevator doors. "Okay." It wasn't really okay with Brian that he was dead, but he didn't know what else to say in the moment.

"And this," Willow motioned to everything outside of the elevator, "is what you would call Hell. However, because you chose to relieve Emerson of his duty at the precise time of your death, you have assumed his responsibilities."

"What on earth are you talking about?" Brian was overwhelmed with an urge to strangle Old Willow. He tried. She removed both of his arms with a sudden snap, followed by a sloppier sound as the flesh ripped away from his torso a bit at the spots where it had formerly been joined to his arms.

This was surprisingly less painful than experiencing the Devil's outrage a moment before, but it was still a very unpleasant experience. Brian tried to intellectualize the whole thing and thought about mentioning that he assumed he would become a soul, detached from his own body when he died but the thought was interrupted by Willow.

"Want'em back?" She held up his arms.

"Yes," Brian said reflexively.

Willow jammed the shoulder ends of the arms into his torso and they reattached with a pop. The whole sequence of events was relatively bloodless but there was certainly a measure of pain to it all.

"We only have a few minutes before the next arrivals, so listen up." Willow was matter of fact in her explanation of the situation, right down to the fact that Brian would never again leave the elevator. He tried to respond and ask questions but there wasn't time. "They're ready."

With those words, Brian felt an extreme pain throughout his entire body, except for his right hand which seemed to involuntarily move in the direction of the elevator panel. He stepped toward the panel.

"That's better." Willow stepped away from the elevator. "Now close the doors and go get them."

Brian was about to ask how he might know what to do next but a deafening voice in his ears told him to close the door. He did. The same voice immediately told him to press the button labelled 32. There was no thirty-second floor in the Ames. Brian sobbed uncontrollably as he pressed the button.

Chapter 20

President Brian McDonald was found dead on the floor of the elevator of the Ames Hotel by Morty Fedelstein. He had been dead for well over an hour before he was found, according to the coroner. No one had gone in or out of the hotel since the President sent Morty and the others away. Immediately after the President was found, Morty and Amy ran the steps up to Flora's apartment, while any sign of foul play in the elevator was ruled out. They knocked on the door together. They told Flora about her father's death and the three of them cried together in the doorway.

Eli heard the sobbing from the room they and Flora used as an office and rushed to the door. Through the tears and shortness of breath they were able to understand what had happened. Eli consoled Flora but shed no tears. They felt bad for those who were crying but had very little sadness over the death of Brian McDonald. It had only been forty-five minutes since Flora had stormed into the office, furious with her father over the vaccine. Eli couldn't help but pick up on the extreme guilt behind Flora's tears. Her final encounter with her father had been awful and he left on bad terms. Eli held Flora compassionately, allowing her to fall into them for comfort. The four of them did not leave the doorway for several minutes.

"I have to see him." Flora cried. "Did anyone tell mom?"

Morty wiped tears from his eyes, "Your mother can't be found right now, Flora, and we can't let you into the elevator yet. They have the whole thing blocked off, but we can go down the stairs."

Flora sprinted toward the stairs and the rest followed.

Police tape surrounded the lobby. Detectives and Secret Service investigators were standing around the President's fallen body. Flora tried to run to him but was held back by an agent. Morty gave the agent a stern look. The chief investigator recognized Flora immediately and gave the okay sign to the agent to let her through. The agent apologized and offered her condolences as Flora quietly knelt beside her father.

"Oh daddy," she sobbed, "daddy, daddy, daddy, I am so sorry." Flora rested her head on her father's chest, smelling his cologne. She tried to crawl inside of his arms like she did when she was younger, but he had fallen with one arm lodged underneath his own weight. Flora raised her eyes to Eli who stroked her hair in comfort. She turned toward the chief investigator, "How?"

"We think a heart attack, miss." The chief investigator could see that Flora was immediately struck by the answer and tried to soothe the shock. "Nothing could have been done, miss. Probably just the stress of dealing with the virus," he said, and only making things worse added, "I can't imagine the pressure. The whole world dying from a virus and he was trying so hard to develop a vaccine."

Flora burst forth with a flood of tears crying, "No, No, No, it was me. I killed him; I killed my daddy!"

Eli and Flora had discussed the vaccine and her father's attempt to inoculate her. Eli knew that Flora had told him off and that she and her father had been upset with one another for months. It was only natural to be blaming herself for his death based on what had transpired. They knew that now was not the time to try to explain that she had nothing to do with his diet, his weight, the fact that he had just recovered from the virus and that it was inevitable that he would suffer a heart attack at some point, given the strain, etc. Instead, they knelt beside her and did what they could saying, "it's going to be okay." Eli helped Flora to her feet, and they left the elevator and then the Ames.

The Vice-President became the President and released the vaccine the very next day. It was named the Brian McDonald Vaccine by the press, who touted him as a savior. No one ever discovered the origin of the virus. Flora received well wishes from people across the world and her mother showed up just in time for the funeral.

Eli, Fitz, and Ella got a bunch of friends together to move everything out of the Ames Hotel. Flora didn't go back to her penthouse apartment at all after seeing and crying over her father's corpse in the elevator.

Eli was struck by the fact that they no longer saw Emerson. The entire time they were moving, Eli made special effort to be alone in the elevator. They were certain that Emerson would have some idea what happened to the President. If it was a simple heart attack, Emerson would have been there to see it. It took a couple of days to clear everything out, but still, no Emerson.

Flora and Eli bought a house in Cambridge and shared it with Ella and Fitz. They rented the other half out to other students for what it cost to maintain.

HOMO had been wrecked by the virus. The momentum for change that had begun before the virus was muffled by masks and political policy remained the same as it had been, divisive and controlling. In response, Eli went back to YouTube full-bore with Flora as a frequent guest host. They also discovered a breakthrough in Flora's organic battery technology that would increase production and guarantee carbon neutral energy in abundance. The ratio of output to input reversed, so the batteries were growing energy.

People of color did not benefit in any way from the efforts they had put into Black Lives Matter and the HOMO movement. All their struggle was reduced to sub headlines and side stories while the virus and its vaccine took center stage. There were a few legitimate reporters still active in the media who exposed the truth about the racial inequity in America. There were some who continued to point out that in addition to the hardship endured simply by being born a person of color, there was a clear and present class division within the country to exacerbate that reality. Eli was one of the people in media who bothered to connect the dots and to keep the focus on the truth. They invited representatives from all the groups who had joined together before the virus to share what was happening in every movement, but still, a moment had been lost due to the virus and the eventual vaccine. People were so happy to walk around in their usual fashion, no longer concerned whether they needed to wear a mask or not, that they behaved as if none of the other, often more life-threatening, societal maladies even existed.

Eli had been broadcasting a live video from the studio at school. They decided they'd visit the Ames Hotel. Eli went there in an attempt to see Emerson.

At the time of Flora's father's death, Eli had been so focused on her that they made no connection to Brian's spirit. Flora didn't like it when they talked to her about the dead. Eli tried hard to remember if they saw Emerson or the President in spirit form at all that day. They were now beginning to believe that just maybe, they had never seen any of it. In fact, they were doubting their own sanity, to a degree, because since Emerson had disappeared, Eli couldn't recall seeing any spirits. They were talking to themselves in a constant stream, reminding themselves of just how many dead people they had actually seen throughout their life and had just decided it was best to shut up and look around, when they realized they had reached the Ames. Eli was about to enter the hotel when they saw a man and a dog walking toward them. They were spirits.

"Emerson?"

"Eli."

"Woof."

"Emerson, you aren't in the elevator. How?" Then it hit them. "You've gotta be kidding me." Eli began to jump up and down which excited Lucille who also popped up and down while howling, yelping and generally carrying on. Eli was laughing, standing six feet from the door of the hotel, by themselves as far as the rest of the world could tell, but they didn't care. "I have a present for you." Eli said excitedly as they reached into their pocket. A slight breeze stirred the flowers in the pot by the hotel entrance and Eli thought better about their next move. "We need to go inside."

"Good to see you, son. This is Lucille," Emerson smiled broadly as he stepped through the doorway Eli held open, "She's happy to see you too. But I'm guessin' you figured that."

Eli was aware of the concierge and wanting to enter unrecognized guided Emerson and Lucille around the other side of a pillar. There, they took a small handkerchief from their pocket and unfolded it. Within lay three golden hairs. "I'm assuming you know what these are?"

Emerson looked at Eli with eyes that welled so deep the pools appeared endless.

Eli picked up a single gold hair and held it out to Emerson. "I believe this will set you free at last. You will no longer be in service to the Devil, in or out of the elevator."

"Thank you m'boy, thank you." Emerson wiped the tears from his cheek as he took the golden hair. Eli looked at Lucille and suddenly felt concern. Emerson could see the apprehension, "It's okay," he smiled and patted his dog's head, "Lucille's with me." As soon as the words left his mouth, Eli could no longer see Emerson or Lucille.

Eli was conflicted. They really wanted to know if what they had guessed was true. Was it possible that Brian McDonald accidentally relieved Emerson of his duty as the elevator operator to Hell? On one hand it would be poetic justice for President Brian McDonald to suffer eternity as an elevator operator, on the other, they knew they had the thing Flora's father needed most. Either way, they decided, they had to know. Eli paced around the lobby for twenty minutes. They didn't want to be the one to press the button and they weren't entirely sure how they would react if they had been correct.

Ding!

Now Eli was truly confused. This was the same ding that happened when Emerson took them to see the Devil's grandmother. This was not the ding that normally happened when one called the elevator at the Ames Hotel; Eli would never forget the difference between the dings. One thing had happened that Eli had not noticed as they paced around indecisively, a woman had appeared just outside of the elevator. She was facing the elevator, so they couldn't see her face, but by her stance, she seemed old. She was wearing an old fur coat. The doors opened to the elevator as Eli attempted to pass quickly to a hidden vantage point. They were, instead, standing in the precise center of the lobby when the doors fully opened, and Brian McDonald saw them.

"What the hell took ya'" the old woman hollered at Brian who was trying to peek around her the whole time she hobbled her way into the elevator. She was a nasty old woman who didn't realize she was going to hell and was apparently unaware that she was beating on a ghost with her handbag. "Get going you big, dumb oaf!" She whacked the elevator operator again.

Eli had never seen the President look so pathetic, but it was clear he had no choice as he closed the doors. Eli thought they had seen Brian McDonald attempt to say something, but it appeared as though he just gave up instead. Eli krew it was now time to tell Flora everything and hope that she agreed there was nothing they could have done differently. They decided to leave it up to Flora to determine whether to give her father the golden hair of the Devil or not. After all, now that they knew the whole thing was real, it made those golden hairs even more valuable. Eli was more inclined to protect just about anyone other than President Brian McDonald from the Devil, if the need arose.

Brian McDonald had given up. It had already seemed like an eternity since his death. He had no willpower, no drive, no sense of humor. It had been beaten out of him by Satan. The first week was awful. Brian had a real hard time adjusting to not being the president and being in the service of the Devil, transporting the souls of those doomed to hell. All of whom treated him like a lowly elevator operator, which he had become. He would argue with them, often fighting, spilling guts and blood everywhere throughout the elevator. Being already dead made the fighting exhausting. There was no such thing as bleeding out. Satan didn't tolerate that sort of behavior from an elevator operator and reminded Brian what ultimate pain feels like every time he misbehaved.

Lucifer explained nothing to Brian. He simply expected Brian to be the elevator operator, opening and closing the door when it was required. The elevator actually told Brian when and where to go, through a series of excruciating signals. The elevator's button panel would reflect the correct number of floors for any given situation. The rest of the time Brian McDonald was alone, in an elevator, with his thoughts of hopeless, fruitless suicide and his memories of what a horrible human being he had been. He was ruminating on his decision to launch the virus when the elevator opened, and he saw Eli. He tried to call out to them, past the old woman, but he was unable to form any words. One thing he was sure of, though, was that Eli could see him.

After he dropped the old bag in hell, Brian McDonald had an exceedingly long time to dwell on his mistakes. He did exactly what Emerson had done before him. However, in Emerson's case, it wasn't as though he had murdered millions and that was just one of Brian's atrocities. It would be quite some time before Brian could even catch a glimpse of what existed beyond the elevator. That is, if it ever revealed itself to him at all.

Emerson had spent decades reviewing his life, examining how he ended up where he had and even though he was still bitter about being stuck in the elevator, he took accountability for his actions. By the time he first met Eli, Emerson had already discovered a world beyond the elevator. It was there that he would go to look for Lucille. He figured out that the elevator pulled him back no matter where he went. Emerson had learned to stop the pain. Once he had completely surrendered to the unalterable fact that he would be spending eternity as the elevator operator to Hell, and acknowledged his part in his own situation, the walls of his prison disappeared. This freedom would not find its way to Brian McDonald anytime soon. Despite being defeated, he still had a long way to go to being repentant.

Flora, on the other hand, was sorry every single day since her father passed away. She was sorry that she couldn't find a way to separate her father from the politics, sorry that she couldn't return to the feelings she had as a little girl, where her daddy was everything to her, and she hadn't yet experienced the reality of human existence.

"I saw your father." Eli blurted out upon their arrival at the apartment where they found Flora, once again, soaked in tears. She looked up at them from the couch, her eyes clouded with sadness. Her look changed to one of confusion as her sorrowful mind was able to process that which Eli had just said.

"You what?"

"I saw him." Eli responded as softly as possible as if the very words would cause what was left of her fragile psyche to crumble onto the apartment floor. They knew they were taking a risk after what had happened when they tried to tell Flora about the trip to Hell and the three golden hairs. Flora had always accepted that Eli believed that they saw dead people. It was something she had chosen to simply go along with since there had never really been any evidence of the veracity of Eli's descriptions, and she was, after all, a practical young woman. She had tried hard to believe Eli's stories of their trip in the elevator, but they described it as lasting for a few days when Eli had only been out for coffee for a maximum of half an hour. The explanation that time has no meaning in the land of the dead was not enough to convince Flora. The three golden hairs Eli produced from their handkerchief were useless when offered as evidence since they looked exactly like those the neighbor's golden retriever shed regularly throughout the Ames Hotel. It didn't help that Eli had always been a bit of a prankster and frequently played tricks on Flora. Eli would have to convince Flora that this was no April Fool's hoax. "I saw his ghost, spirit, whatever it is I see." Eli had never become comfortable with seeing the dead but did very little to let those around themselves know how difficult it was to parse the living from the dead. Eli had no control over it, and some days were worse than others. "Flora, love, I should have done more to understand this thing I can do. But, Babe, it's hard enough to understand the living."

"So, he's really dead," Flora sobbed, "and you saw him somewhere, dead?"

"Well, yeah, y'know the way I see people dead, which is more like living," Eli did their best to explain themselves, "like, walking and talking, usually complaining about why they are dead or how they got dead if they bother to talk to me." Eli could tell they were flubbing and chose to redirect, "the point being that I saw your father standing in our elevator at the Ames. Whatever you want to say to him I can say for you."

Flora wiped her eyes and stood up. She kissed Eli gratefully and held their head between her palms, "you can really talk to dead people, can't you?"

"Yes, I can."

"Let's go talk to my dead daddy." Flora released Eli with another kiss, grabbed her keys from the cabinet by the front door and waited for Eli to get the hint.

A short bus ride from Cambridge and a bit of walking brought Flora and Eli to the front doors of the Ames Hotel. A hard mix of emotions rushed over Flora as she remembered the good times they had together, then the vision of her father, dead in the elevator. If what Eli had seen was real, the ghost of her daddy was now damned to an eternity of servitude as the elevator operator to Hell.

"It's going to be okay," Eli reassured Flora, "you don't have to make a decision today." They had talked about the golden hairs Eli still had in the handkerchief on the bus ride. Eli had explained the options. They could give her father a golden hair and with it the power to release himself from the control the Devil had on his soul, or they could punish him for his crimes against humanity, of which they both agreed were many. Eli was quick to follow up with, "But he is your daddy!"

"Yes, he is, and I am going to release him." Flora strapped on a look of full commitment, "But not until he apologizes," she turned to Eli, "you will be able to hear him apologize, right?" without waiting for a response she marched her way through the entrance.

"Flora," the concierge called out, inaudible in Flora's bubble of commitment.

"Hi, Chloe, we are kinda…" Eli pointed toward the elevator. Flora had pushed the button.

Ding!

The elevator doors opened, and Eli could see the President, who immediately burst into tears at the sight of Flora. She was clinging to Eli, judging their expression before they had time to tell her what they were seeing, and she looked toward the spot where Eli's eyes told her that daddy would be standing. The living and the dead attempted to hug. It was the saddest and most comical thing anyone who witnessed it would ever see, which boiled down to Eli and Chloe at the front desk.

"Where is he?" Flora cried as she looped her arms around elevator air.

Even though Brian McDonald could see her, he couldn't tell when his own hands met her actual, real, solid body. He had been doing the job for long enough now that the conundrum of how he might be able to operate the elevator, pressing buttons that felt like real buttons and at the same time be incapable of touching the occasional living humans who entered his elevator cab, no longer held his interest. However, it occurred to him that what he might have gleaned from further investigation had he chosen to pursue it may have come in handy in the moment. So, he fumbled badly, crying the entire time. Only Eli could see and feel everyone involved so they pushed daughter and daddy out of each other's personal space. "There, now you are together but separate. Flora, your daddy is here, and he is crying."

"Tell her I love her." "Tell him I miss him."

"One at a time, please." Eli asked as they looked at Flora. Brian McDonald waited to hear what Flora had to say.

"I miss you so much daddy. I love you." Flora said with relief as Eli waited for Brian's reply.

"I can't hear her," he said. Brian McDonald was smart, even in death. He had mastered what he could do with the elevator, everything except how to leave it. One of the things he had learned how to do with the elevator was to haunt it. He quickly closed the doors and instantly Eli could hear Brian more clearly. Flora's head whipped upward. She thought she heard an echo of her father's voice.

"Daddy?"

"Flora, can you hear me?" Brian didn't need a response as Flora folded over and wept. "There, there, my darling, it's okay, daddy's here." Brian crumpled to the floor and sobbed.

Eli found themselves tucking in-between the two, serving as a sort of comfort bridge between the living and the dead. The President had never hugged them while alive and the whole thing was truly bizarre. Then it got worse.

"I'm sorry," Brian McDonald finally said after he had cried himself out on Eli's shoulder.

"Oh, daddy, don't." Flora wrapped her arm around Eli, using their arm to press into her father's shoulders as they all sat in a heap on the floor of the elevator. "I'm just so happy to hear your voice. Say something more, anything more, but don't be sorry."

"Flora. I know how this happened to me." Brian tried to explain what had happened, as much for himself as for Flora. "I brought it on myself. I did terrible things."

In that moment, Flora didn't want the truth. "I don't want to hear it daddy. I just want to hear you."

It was both terribly sweet and awkward over the following hour and a half as the President fell way to the father and the father melted into the daddy Flora remembered from her childhood. Eli was a good puppet and a good listener as daddy and daughter used their limbs as extensions of their respective emotions, until Brian let go of their arm and stood up. Flora could feel Eli's whole body shift from the change as she lost the physical connection to her father.

"Flora," Brian knew that this might be the only time for him to be the one to tell her the truth about the virus and his hand in its release. "Eli, both of you. In fact, everyone. This is for everyone." Eli tried to translate with their own eyes the expression upon Brian's face. Flora understood the gravity behind the voice. "I have committed an atrocity. And it's far worse than waiting too long to come around on climate, which, since I am being honest, I really didn't do, but that's a different story."

The silence was agonizing as Brian tried to summon the courage to finally speak the truth. Eli did their able best to reflect the posture and manner of Brian McDonald who looked more sincere in this moment than Eli had ever seen him.

"I caused the virus."

Eli and Flora stood staring at one another, at first out of incredulity, then out of fear, then out of realization as Eli confirmed that the President stood crying in the corner of the elevator, his contrition apparent. They did their best to act as expression translator to the dead through their own realization of what had transpired.

"I killed millions of people across the world to satisfy my own political motives." Brian McDonald was confessing to global murder of a different kind than society had come to accept. He could see Flora's expression had turned back to that of the woman she had become, a woman who put the people before herself and that woman was angry.

"You horrible beast!" Flora hollered as she rushed the place Eli's eyes told her the ghost of her deceased father was cowering in shame and regret. She slammed her fists into the walls of the elevator cab with resounding thuds. "How could you? How could anyone?" She pounded and pounded and pounded, as if she could remove the painful truth by hammering it out of the walls. "I hate you!" Flora deflated entirely. Her sobbing body heaved with each breath.

"I hate myself." Brian barely spoke. "It's the only thing I think of. I don't even pay attention to all the souls I transport every day. I think of all those who died because of me. But mostly, I think of all those they leave behind. And then, I think of you, Flora. I think of how you showed me just how wrong I had been. I wanted to save you from what I had done. Even though you had no idea I was behind it, you still, when given the chance to protect yourself, chose to protect others first." Brian McDonald knew he could not repair the damage he had done to the world, but he hoped for the opportunity to love his daughter and for her to understand that the love he felt for her was real and honest.

Eli laughed. It was unexpected for all. Eli hadn't intended to laugh. Eli wasn't feeling particularly jubilant or even remotely amused. Eli was almost as upset as she was by the news that Flora's father was a whole different class of murderer than they had understood him to be before walking into the elevator. However, Eli often experienced the inability to diffuse an outburst over irony and they had just slipped their hand into the pocket with the handkerchief.

"I'm sorry, I didn't mean to laugh. It's just. Never mind." Eli decided the situation was too grave and that the explanation wouldn't fly. They left the handkerchief in their pocket and leaned over to stroke Flora's hair.

"It's the handkerchief, Eli, isn't it?" Flora said from a sudden calm. She smiled and let out the faintest breath of a laugh as she looked in the direction, she assumed her father to be. "And he doesn't know." Flora checked Eli to confirm. Brian was deer in the headlights. "Well, we came here to forgive him. Now, it's simply up to us to decide, if, after further review of new information as to the level of maniac that was my father, whether or not we can still extend that forgiveness."

"I am more than sorry, Flora, Eli. Your forgiveness is all that I can hope for." Brian McDonald was clearer than he had ever felt. The crippling anguish of hours and hours reliving his bad decisions, alone in the elevator, had left him with one thought. "The only good thing I have ever done in my entire life is to have loved you." As he said it, Brian realized, he did love Eli. He had done nearly everything he could to separate her from the most important person in her life and in the end, he had strengthened that bond, rather than broken it. For every selfish and manipulative action he had taken, Eli stood on the opposite side, the side Flora stood on. Brian had come to realize that all of the things he had valued in life, things he thought were right, things like money, control and power, were meaningless. He had missed out on sharing, acceptance, and most of all, love. And the place he saw love most clearly shown was between Eli and his daughter Flora. In that moment Brian found that true love. "I hope I haven't ruined the world, especially for the two of you. And even though I know what I have to say about it isn't important, if you two ever decide to get married, I give you my blessing."

Gong!

Brian McDonald had no choice but to do his job and open the elevator doors and there was only one way that the elevator would go anywhere without him knowing it. Also, the gong was always a dead giveaway.

"HELLO." The Devil smiled in self-satisfaction.

Brian McDonald turned to look at Flora and Eli who were transfixed by the Devil. He turned back to the Devil and said, "hello."

"Not you stupid." The Devil stepped into the elevator but felt a sudden chill. "Ooh, what the fuck is that?" The chill was so uncomfortable the Devil stepped back out of the elevator.

"I see you met Eli," the Devil's grandmother's voice rang from the staircase.

Flora hadn't the time to take in what was happening as everything that Eli had described presented itself to her in the space of a minute. Eli tilted their head as if the action would make the mind adjust to the reality. It didn't.

"Come, come, let's discuss." Willow was radiant and Lucifer was beside himself. Willow motioned to them to come toward her and all were obedient. Brian McDonald did not try to step forward. He had been conditioned and was obedient. "You too, McDonald," Willow continued to motion with her hands, "c'mon, c'mon, but just for the chat."

Brian McDonald stepped off of the elevator for the first time since he had died. He walked toward Willow, down the staircase he had only seen the top of, following his daughter accompanied by her one true love and Lucifer. It was bizarre and oddly beautiful.

"It's time for you to decide." Willow stood directly in front of Flora who had still not fully comprehended where she was and who the beautiful older woman was. She was battling with the recognition that despite being devilishly handsome, the Devil was somehow intimidated by Eli and controlled by this woman. Being asked to decide something in the middle of this seemed out of the question.

"What's the question?" Flora asked rather aimlessly.

"Are you giving daddy a golden hair or not?" Willow said frankly.

"Um, okay, so that whole thing. The Devil. The golden hairs. The dream. All of it, is real?" Flora was coming around.

"Yes, very real, Flora. And your father, well, your father is a real piece of shit." Willow answered, again, frankly.

"Leading the witness!" Lucifer raised his hand up in the air and brought down a gavel that appeared from nowhere for a mighty crash on the arm of his throne. It shook the place.

"She's the judge, Lucy. Stay out of it." Willow turned to Flora, "Are you going to give a golden hair to your daddy, so he is no longer in service to my Lucifer?" Willow was beautiful and patient, but she

195

had limits, "Suspense is killing us," Willow chuckled, "well, not technically, but just the same. Grams got business elsewhere if y'know what I mean."

Flora's eyes swelled with tears as she fully realized she held her daddy's immortal soul in her hands. She didn't know if she had the right, but she was clearly being given it. She looked at Brian who despite finally being able to look around at something other than the four walls of his eternal prison was focused on her. His eyes appeared warm, gentle and loving, like she always wanted to remember them.

"Yes." Flora nodded to Eli who opened his handkerchief and handed one of the hairs to Brian.

Brian held the hair tightly between thumb and forefinger and walked it over to Satan who took it slowly and regrettably.

"And I'll be wanting my pen." The Devil held his hand out.

Brian reached his hand into his breast pocket to find that, indeed, he still had the gold pen the Devil had given him. He handed it to the Devil.

"Fine," the Devil rose from his throne, "debt paid; you win the bet Grams." The Devil walked directly through the windows to his place of solace, the writhing mass of tortured human souls that were now a part of him, one less was forgotten as quickly as it was lost.

Brian McDonald breathed a sigh of relief and became visible to Flora. She dove at him, half-expecting to fall through him but he was solid. They hugged for a very long time until Brian extended an arm toward Eli who also fell into the warmth of pure love and forgiveness.

"That's enough," Willow's voice pulled the three up from their hug. They were back in the elevator. "Up," Willow commanded, and Brian found that he had no choice but to follow. Willow looked at each of the three stunned faces and laughed a little. "What? You didn't think he'd get off Scot free did yah?" It was clear to Willow that they weren't catching on. "I am not forgiving you for what you have done. You are still bound to me. I control the elevator, among a few other things." As Willow spoke, she pulled back her hair, three golden hairs shined with an inner radiance that was impossible to look at, even for the dead. "I have given you one last opportunity to be with one another because of the profound forgiveness you have shown, Flora McDonald. As far as you go Brian, I will retain your services until you are freed, and I have nothing to say about how that happens. Maybe Eli will share the secret someday, but I would prefer not. I will allow you to continue to see your father, Flora, for as long as he is in service to me."

"Are you God?" Eli asked.

"Oh, Heavens no. I'm their grandmother."

The end

The Tale

The Devil and the Three Golden Hairs

By the Brothers Grimm

There was once a poor woman who gave birth to a little son, and as he came into the world with a caul on, it was predicted that in his fourteenth year he would have the king's daughter for his wife. It happened that soon afterwards the king came into the village, and no one knew that he was the king, and when he asked the people what news there was, they answered, a child has just been born with a caul on, whatever anyone so born undertakes turns out well. It is prophesied, too, that in his fourteenth year he will have the king's daughter for his wife.

The king, who had a bad heart, and was angry about the prophecy, went to the parents, and, seeming quite friendly, said, you poor people, let me have your child, and I will take care of it. At first they refused, but when the stranger offered them a large amount of gold for it, and they thought, it is a child of good fortune, and everything must turn out well for it, they at last consented, and gave him the child.

The king put it in a box and rode away with it until he came to a deep piece of water, then he threw the box into it and thought, I have freed my daughter from her undesired suitor.

The box, however, did not sink, but floated like a boat, and not a drop of water made its way into it. And it floated to within two miles of the king's chief city, where there was a mill, and it came to a halt at the milldam. A miller's boy, who by good luck was standing there, noticed it and pulled it out with a hook, thinking that he had found a great treasure, but when he opened it there lay a pretty boy inside, quite fresh and lively. He took him to the miller and his wife, and as they had no children, they were glad, and said, "God has given him to us." They took great care of the foundling, and he grew up in all goodness.

It happened that once in a storm, the king went into the mill, and asked the mill-folk if the tall youth were their son. No, answered they, he's a foundling. Fourteen years ago, he floated down to the milldam in a box, and the mill-boy pulled him out of the water.

Then the king knew that it was none other than the child of good fortune which he had thrown into the water, and he said, my good people, could not the youth take a letter to the queen. I will give him two gold pieces as a reward. Just as the king commands, answered they, and they told the boy to hold himself in readiness. Then the king wrote a letter to the queen, wherein he said, as soon as the boy arrives with this letter, let him be killed and buried, and all must be done before I come home. The boy set out with this letter, but he lost his way, and in the evening came to a large forest. In the darkness he saw a small light, he went towards it and reached a cottage. When he went in, an old woman was sitting by the fire quite alone. She started when she saw the boy, and said, whence do you come, and whither are you going. I come from the mill, he answered, and wish to go to the queen, to whom I am taking a letter, but as I have lost my way in the forest I should like to stay here over night. You poor boy, said the woman, you have come into a den of thieves, and when they come home, they will kill you. Let them come, said the boy, I am not afraid, but I am so tired that I cannot go any farther. And he stretched himself upon a bench and fell asleep.

Soon afterwards the robbers came, and angrily asked what strange boy was lying there. Ah, said the old woman, it is an innocent child who has lost himself in the forest, and out of pity I have let him come in, he has to take a letter to the queen. The robbers opened the letter and read it, and in it was written that the boy as soon as he arrived should be put to death. Then the hardhearted robbers felt pity, and their leader tore up the letter and wrote another, saying, that as soon as the boy came, he should be married at once to the king's daughter. Then they let him lie quietly on the bench until the next morning, and when he awoke, they gave him the letter, and showed him the right way.

And the queen, when she had received the letter and read it, did as was written in it, and had a splendid wedding-feast prepared, and the king's daughter was married to the child of good fortune, and as the youth was handsome and friendly she lived with him in joy and contentment.

After some time, the king returned to his palace and saw that the prophecy was fulfilled, and the child married to his daughter. How has that come to pass, said he, I gave quite another order in my letter.

So, the queen gave him the letter, and said that he might see for himself what was written in it. The king read the letter and saw quite well that it had been exchanged for the other. He asked the youth what had become of the letter entrusted to him, and why he had brought another instead of it. I know nothing about it, answered he, it must have been changed in the night, when I slept in the forest. The king said in a passion, you shall not have everything quite so much your own way, whosoever marries my daughter must fetch me from hell three golden hairs from the head of the devil, bring me what I want, and you shall keep my daughter. In this way the king hoped to be rid of him forever. But the child of good fortune answered, I will fetch the golden hairs, I am not afraid of the devil. Whereupon he took leave of them and began his journey.

The road led him to a large town, where the watchman by the gates asked him what his trade was, and what he knew. I know everything, answered the child of good fortune. Then you can do us a favor, said the watchman, if you will tell us why our market fountain, which once flowed with wine has become dry, and no longer gives even water. That you shall know, answered he, only wait until I come back.

Then he went farther and came to another town, and there also the gatekeeper asked him what his trade was, and what he knew. I know everything, answered he. Then you can do us a favor and tell us why a tree in our town which once bore golden apples now does not even put forth leaves. You shall know that, answered he, only wait until I come back.

Then he went on and came to a wide river over which he must cross. The ferryman asked him what his trade was, and what he knew. I know everything, answered he. Then you can do me a favor, said the ferryman, and tell me why I must always be rowing backwards and forwards, and am never set free. You shall know that, answered he, only wait until I come back.

When he had crossed the water, he found the entrance to hell. It was black and sooty within, and the devil was not at home, but his grandmother was sitting in a large armchair. What do you want, said she to him, but she did not look so very wicked. I should like to have three golden hairs from the devil's head, answered he, else I cannot keep my wife. That is a good deal to ask for, said she, if the devil comes home and finds you, it will cost you your life, but as I pity you, I will see if I cannot help you.

She changed him into an ant and said, creep into the folds of my dress, you will be safe there. Yes, answered he, so far, so good, but there are three things besides that I want to know - why a fountain which once flowed with wine has become dry, and no longer gives even water, why a tree which once bore golden apples does not even put forth leaves, and why a ferryman must always be going backwards and forwards, and is never set free. Those are difficult questions, answered she, but just be silent and quiet and pay attention to what the devil says when I pull out the three golden hairs.

As the evening came on, the devil returned home. No sooner had he entered than he noticed that the air was not pure. I smell man's flesh, said he, all is not right here. Then he pried into every corner, and searched, but could not find anything. His grandmother scolded him. It has just been swept, said she, and everything put in order, and now you are upsetting it again, you have always got man's flesh in your nose. Sit down and eat your supper.

When he had eaten and drunk, he was tired and laid his head in his grandmother's lap and told her she should louse him a little. It was not long before he was fast asleep, snoring and breathing heavily. Then the old woman took hold of a golden hair, pulled it out, and laid it down beside her. Oh, cried the devil, what are you doing. I have had a bad dream, answered the grandmother, so I seized hold of your hair. What did you dream then, said the devil. I dreamt that a fountain in a marketplace from which wine once flowed was dried up, and not even water would flow out of it - what is the cause of it. Oh, ho, if they did but know it, answered the devil, there is a toad sitting under a stone in the well - if they killed it, the wine would flow again.

The grandmother loused him again until he went to sleep and snored so that the windows shook. Then she pulled the second hair out. Ha, what are you doing, cried the devil angrily. Do not take it ill, said she, I did it in a dream. What have you dreamt this time, asked he. I dreamt that in a certain kingdom there stood an apple-tree which had once borne golden apples, but now would not even bear leaves. What, think you, was the reason. Oh, if they did but know, answered the devil. A mouse is gnawing at the root - if they killed it, they would have golden apples again, but if it gnaws much longer the tree will wither altogether. But I have had enough of your dreams, if you disturb me in my sleep again you will get a box on the ear.

The grandmother spoke gently to him and picked his lice once more until he fell asleep and snored. Then she took hold of the third golden hair and pulled it out. The devil jumped up, roared out, and would have treated her ill if she had not quieted him again and said, who can help bad dreams. What was the dream, then, asked he, and was quite curious. I dreamt of a ferryman who complained that he must always ferry from one side to the other and was never released. What is the cause of it? Ah, the fool, answered the devil, when anyone comes and wants to go across, he must put the oar in his hand, and the other man will have to ferry, and he will be free. As the grandmother had plucked out the three golden hairs, and the three questions were answered, she let the old devil alone, and he slept until daybreak.

When the devil had gone out again the old woman took the ant out of the folds of her dress and gave the child of good fortune his human shape again. There are the three golden hairs for you, said she. What the devil said to your three questions, I suppose you heard. Yes, answered he, I heard, and will take care to remember. You have what you want, said she, and now you can go your way. He thanked the old woman for helping him in his need, and left hell well content that everything had turned out so fortunately.

When he came to the ferryman, he was expected to give the promised answer. Ferry me across first, said the child of good fortune, and then I will tell you how you can be set free, and when he reached the opposite shore, he gave him the devil's advice. Next time anyone comes, who wants to be ferried over, just put the oar in his hand.

He went on and came to the town wherein stood the unfruitful tree, and there too the watchman wanted an answer. So, he told him what he had heard from the devil. Kill the mouse which is gnawing at its root, and it will again bear golden apples. Then the watchman thanked him and gave him as a reward two asses laden with gold, which followed him.

Finally, he came to the town whose well was dry. He told the watchman what the devil had said, a toad is in the well beneath a stone, you must find it and kill it, and the well will again give wine in plenty. The watchman thanked him, and also gave him two asses laden with gold.

At last, the child of good fortune got home to his wife, who was heartily glad to see him again, and to hear how well he had prospered in everything. To the king he took what he had asked for, the devil's three golden hairs, and when the king saw the four asses laden with gold he was quite content, and said, now all the conditions are fulfilled, and you can keep my daughter.

But tell me, dear son-in-law, where did all that gold come from - this is tremendous wealth. I was rowed across a river, answered he, and got it there, it lies on the shore instead of sand. Can I too fetch some of it, said the king, and he was quite eager about it. As much as you like, answered he.

There is a ferryman on the river, let him ferry you over, and you can fill your sacks on the other side. The greedy king set out in all haste, and when he came to the river, he beckoned to the ferryman to put him across. The ferryman came and bade him get in, and when they got to the other shore, he put the oar in his hand and sprang over. But from this time forth the king had to ferry, as a punishment for his sins. Perhaps he is ferrying still. If he is, it is because no one has taken the oar from him.

*****

www.ingramcontent.com/pod-product-compliance
Lightning Source LLC
Chambersburg PA
CBHW051953220626
47052CB00004B/923